Suicide

Blonde

Darcey

Steinke

THE ATLANTIC MONTHLY PRESS
NEW YORK

Published simultaneously in Canada
Printed in the United States of America
FIRST EDITION

Library of Congress Cataloging-in-Publication Data

Steinke, Darcey.
    Suicide blonde / Darcey Steinke.—1st ed.
    ISBN 0-87113-479-9
    I. Title.
    PS3569.T37924S85   1992   813'.54—dc20   92-3754

Design by Laura Hough
Epigraph by Bill Rutherford © 1992

The Atlantic Monthly Press
19 Union Square West
New York, NY 10003

First printing

Suicide
Blonde

Chapter

One

WAS IT THE BOURBON OR THE DYE FUMES THAT MADE THE PINK walls quiver like vaginal lips? An acidy scent ribboned the pawed tub, fingered up the shower curtain. My vision was liquid and various as a lava lamp. In the mirror I saw the scar from the blackberry bramble that had caught my chin and scratched a hairline curve to my forehead. It was hardly noticeable, but left the impression that my face was cracked. Taking another sip of bourbon, I put on the plastic gloves and began parting my hair at the roots. As the dye snaked out there was a faint sucking sound, like soil pulling water, and I wondered: if I were brave enough to slit my wrists would I bother to dye my hair?

This is what happened: all day yesterday Bell had stared out the window, smoking cigarettes. There were his usual reasons—his father, no acting jobs, that he was getting ugly and old. Plus there was Kevin to moon over. He eyed the eggshell envelope of Kevin's wedding invitation and stared out the window for hours, his face vaguely twitching as he moved from one memory to the next. His melancholy made me think he was getting sick of living with me. And this, in turn, made me want to please him, to show him I was not one of his worries. So when he went walking I put on my black teddy and arranged myself on the futon. Looking at my breasts covered in lace flowers, I thought I seemed overly anxious, like a Danish or a little excitable dog. I looked desperate . . . using the one thing that would keep him near. It seemed manipulative, even if it was an attempt to jerk him from his melancholy. Men are never more appealing than when they brood.

Bell came in and walked to the foot of the bed. His eyes narrowed with lusty admiration for my forwardness. He lay over me and said, "I'm in charge now." But when he didn't release his weight I asked him if he was going to take off his clothes. "You seem to want me to," he said. I blushed and asked him if he felt bullied, told him now he knew how women felt. "You take off that," he said, stretching the lace of the teddy. I rolled it down and then adamantly pulled his shirt off. There was something hard in me that wanted him, no matter how awkward it was going to be. We kissed in a distracted way. Eventually, he turned his head, as if watching a bird move across the horizon. I saw dark continents under the paint of the walls beyond his profile.

"I'm bored," he said.

I sat up on the edge of the bed, then walked to the closet. Shifting the hanging clothes, I felt my hands already beginning to shake. I dressed and went into the kitchen. There was a taste of pennies in my mouth, a fierce nausea and tinny rawness, like the moment after you break a bone.

Bell sat in the dark at the painted table by the window. Occasionally the streetlight would show a wisp of cigarette smoke, his face dissected by crossing panes of light, his eyes clear and vacant like a cat's.

"I have to get more cigarettes," he said.

He didn't sound mean, just sullen. And I couldn't tell whether he was falling clunkily out of love with me, or if, as he claimed, it was just his usual reticence. Sometimes I suspected he was stunted, not capable of predictable human emotions. Last week he had laughed at a tourist couple separated by the BART train doors. I imagined a wire grid behind the skin of his forehead and a cold metallic look in his eyes. Of course it was only my imagination, but the sensation was terrifying, like finding out your lover is a killer.

Now he'd been gone twenty-four hours. For a while I had found his habit of floating off charming, but to appreciate this suddenly seemed masochistic. I didn't want to be one of those women addicted to indifference.

I peeled down my gloves and threw them gingerly, like used condoms, into the trash. The teddy incident was terrifying because it exacerbated the sensation that my feminine power was diminishing, trickling like drops of milk from a leaky pitcher. I wrapped my hair in a towel. The way I looked reminded me of some clichéd floundering female, so I took off my robe and lay across the couch, a better spot to watch shadows gather in the fleshy green fingers of the big jade plant. He'd inherited it from the last inhabitants of the apartment, because it wouldn't fit through the door when they moved. Near the plant was a cedar wall panel with a Japanese scene. Bell's boa hung on a hook beside his film stills; blurry body gestures from a super-8 film Bell made years ago. There were lots of little things: the blue glass lamp, the leopard with eyes that glowed, empty wine bottles, brass goblets, postcards of Europe from former lovers, candles and incense on a special table with a linen cloth, along with Bell's crucifixes, saints, Hindu gods, a GI Joe doll, obsidian voodoo beads, a dog's skull and an African mask of an antelope.

The window looked over Bush Street and toward the staggered roofs of Nob Hill, slanted like some Middle Eastern capital. The penthouse terraces had exotic French doors, miniature lemon trees and lacy wrought-iron furniture. On one there was a green fountain; another, on warm days, had a stand with a cockatiel. Above it all shone the neon Hotel Huntington sign, drenching our room with wavering green light.

My body was like a part of the room, a chair or a vase. I remembered the first time I saw my mother naked. She stood before a mirror, pulled at her hips, pressing her stomach, checking as I was now for signs of decay. The female body, I thought, has the capacity for such exquisiteness and such horror. I sat up to drink, but the bourbon spilled and trickled over my breasts, running all the way down to form a puddle in my navel.

Watching my body I had the sensation it was the same as Bell's. Images came fast: an expressive hand gesture, his smell—wet dirt and hand-rolled cigarettes—how his features were large and most beautiful when he was meditative, how in certain light his skin paled so that it looked blue, how he seemed at those times like a creature and I half expected to see wings appear on his shoulder blades.

In temperament Bell was not so much exotic as sophisticatedly adolescent. He had intellectualized youth's themes, perfected and lyricized them. And this core of exquisite longing was his excuse for brooding, for his erratic behavior, and the fuel for his philosophy of life's emptiness and the cult of pleasure. But Bell wasn't really immature, just trapped in some premature state, like a beetle whose back is all the more vivid because the last homogenizing stage to adulthood is never reached.

The clock ticked loud; it seemed to mock me with its pointy fingers and monotonous rhythyms. I took a swig from the bottle and realized I was drunk. My thoughts were jagged and I had the sensation that my life was exactly half over. It started with a tingle in the back of my skull that made me shiver, then spread over my head like a hood. But I've never felt any different. And I knew my memories, childhood or otherwise, were simply times I rose up into consciousness and was intensely myself. I heard the hum I always do when a memory is encasing itself and I recognized that sound as my particular and continual way of being alive.

My hair stunk up the whole apartment. I cracked the window and Bell's boa expanded with air. In the bathroom, the porcelain tub was cool to the touch. I adjusted the water, pulled the towel from my head and then got in, kneeling on all fours. My breasts swung down, reminding me of the utilitarian tits of mammals. And through the scope of cleavage I could see the hair between my thighs. The tiny black curls seemed scrawny, even obscene. Water beat on my hair. The bleach was strong. My face became prickly and warm and I realized that even though I was alone, I felt embarrassed. The acidic residue backed up, biting into my knees. *I am dyeing my hair to get Bell back,* I thought, *and because the whole world loves a blonde.* The bright light made the room stark, soap flecked into my eyes and I felt a rising frazzled sensation that always means I'm going to cry. The water ran clear down the drain. When I stood, my hair was steaming, tangled together in clumps like pale shiny snakes.

I moved, dripping through the dark apartment, to the window. The hotel sign blazing through the evening fog. Its aura occasionally flared out like a sunspot and I could feel the power spark into me through the thousand roots of my scalp, each one now flaunting a golden hair.

THE BRASS DOOR OF THE APARTMENT BUILDING SUCKED SHUT behind me. The night was balmy. I heard the bells of Grace Cathedral, thought of going there, sitting in a back pew, the bloodied light over me, heady as a red-wine buzz. Jesus would be everywhere in radiant stained glass, his face over and over like a man you loved or one you had killed. Bush Street was so steep I had to lean back slightly, which made the comforting city minutiae—the lanternish lights of Pacific Heights, the quiltlike Victorians and the sculptured bushes—seem distant. I held my arms forward to stop this sensation, then quickly let them fall, the gesture seemed crazy.

Maybe I shouldn't search for Bell, but to stay in the apartment was impossible. What did it mean that I wasn't the kind of girl who could wait, dispassionately passing time drinking wine or reading a novel? My instincts told me to leave him, it's what I always did when I sensed the first soft spot of discontent. I was the kind of girl who left men. It wasn't like me to look for Bell. And I knew searching was no different than putting on the teddy or dyeing my hair. I thought of my mother, how when my father threatened to leave her, she started to take longer to get ready and always wore a bright shade of red lipstick . . . suddenly she was working so hard to be loved.

At first the nights were cozy, I'd make soup and we'd lounge on the bed reading the paper, the radiator crackling. The night was distinctly outside and we were safe in its center. Now, the night is like poisonous gas and infiltrates every room. And Bell, like a whore or a junkie, has changed day into night. My love has splintered, so I saw him everywhere. Inside storefronts and bars, in the shiny elongated cars, even in the eyes of a big-assed woman in pink pants, and a tall thin man with a shaggy mustache like a Texas cowboy. The bourbon exacerbated Polk Street's seedy carnival ambience.

The Motherlode was much like other gay bars on the block, filled with men in casual clothes. The disco music was so loud it shivered the glass. Most watched the large video screen showing a man on all fours on top of a bar, a leather monster, with a little chauffeur's cap and a black leather vest. His pants were around his knees. An identical man was jerking his fist into the first man's anus. The crowd watched, but no one seemed particularly interested. Instead of arousing the men, it seemed to make them shy, and together with the bar's decoration— crepe paper and silver stars—the place had the atmosphere of prom night.

On the corner, a covey of young men waited between windows filled with vinyl shower curtains, sensuous as tongues. All were thin as eels and there was one peroxide blond with a complexion so puckered it resembled the surface of the moon.

His hips were pressed forward and he wore a leather belt with straps circling his thighs. I couldn't help staring, there was something puffed up and trembling about him. He caught me looking and said, "I wouldn't sleep with that," and flipped his chin toward me. There was a riff of laughter from the others. I tried to avoid them, but the blond stepped forward and nudged me, startled me enough so I lost my balance and stumbled toward the glittery cement. When I tried to stand he thrust his hips into my face. My lips brushed the grainy texture of his jeans. He laughed, his head haloed by the moon.

I stood, ran. My face burned and I yelled, "Assholes!" and the blond camped back, "For sale!"

My teeth clenched and there was that shifting and shaky feeling again. I was terrified that Bell was going back to the boys.

* * *

THE BLACK ROSE HAD A POSTAPOCALYPTIC FEEL, AS IF BURNT
out and only marginally re-established. The interior was black
with low ceilings and any light was random and murky. I noticed particularly the metal cone fireplace and how the bartender stoked and tended the fire diligently, as if his were the
last embers on earth. It wasn't a gay bar like most of the
places off Polk Street, but there was a smattering of queens
among the punks with nose rings and ruddy-cheeked old-tim-
ers at the bar. All of them, as well as the people in the deep
booths and at the carved tables in back, came for the cheap
beer. A screamy song blasted from the jukebox. And though I
came to wait for Bell, because he had a drink at the Black
Rose every night, I was relieved he wasn't here. What would I
say? I felt strange for pursuing such an awkward situation. I
thought of crazy things: I would walk up to him and tell him
my mother died, I would say an old boyfriend called, tell him
a magazine wanted my photographs or maybe go all the way
and pretend to be pregnant.

But I hated myself for thinking like that. Why should I
need anything interesting or provocative to say? It reminded me
of the sudden and forced interest my mother took in my father's
middle-aged hobbies after he threatened to leave, of how once
in the car searching for the church softball game she almost
started to cry because we couldn't find the playing field.

I ordered a bourbon and sat in the back. Scribbling on
my napkin I wrote, *Just give me back this one,* then *Love is not
based on worth* and *No one is dying from this.* I wrote and
rewrote that, and because it was true I felt overly dramatic, even

stupid. I realized I was writing phrases with a vague thought that Bell would see them. The idea that everything I did was generated by him made me feel dismal.

Why was Bell so dissolute? When I confronted him on his wanderings, he would say I was selfish to think I was responsible. It had to do with his father, he'd say, how motionless his face had been the moment he died, how the slack skin around his chin reminded Bell of his own loosening flesh. "Do you know how terrible it is to wear the skin of a dead man?" he would say.

Bell came in then, followed by a young man. I knew I wouldn't speak to him. He was intimidating, even stellar. At first I thought the young man was Kevin, but he was one of Bell's old lovers. Kevin was older now, and besides he lived in Los Angeles and was getting married soon. On closer look, the man was tiny, not young. He had red hair and a quick satyric way of moving.

Bell looked exhausted, hallowed and light, almost weightless. They sat at a far table, the little man toward me and Bell in profile. I couldn't hear what they said, but it was easy enough to see their faces, though they couldn't see mine. I read their expressions as if I were reading the ingredients of a bottle of poison I swallowed by mistake. Bell's concentration and ease made me shiver. It reminded me of our first dreamy months, when he teased me playfully without malice, when our moral structure seemed identical. But these same gestures were ominous now. And there was a growing leisure to his movements that made him seem disinterested in whatever the little man was saying. He was acting, as he always did, resistant, withholding. In bed Bell would lean his bare shoulders up against the wall, always waiting for me to come to him. The little man talked with his mouth wide open and gesticulated with his chin. After every statement he stopped and looked intensely into Bell's face.

Bell gazed off, blew long indifferent tendrils of smoke. This discourse was beginning to look like an interrogation. Bell rebuked, and I knew that then he spoke about his latest idea, that no one ever had an original idea, any notion was a confluence of news, former ideas, history, music, and you were just one of many who pulled it down out of the air. The little man was chastised, cast his eyes down, then grabbed Bell's wrist. He twisted it back and said something urgent.

Bell loosened the little man's arm, lit a cigarette and walked to the door. He looked my way though he didn't see me. I could tell by his insular expression that he thought of me and would soon be coming home.

The little man ordered another drink, he kept looking at the door and silently moving his lips. I thought of comforting him, explaining that Bell was always like that, you couldn't expect him to listen to logic, he was a surrealist. I'd tell him about the strange still lifes I sometimes woke to, a single black high heel, a brown egg, long thick nails scattered around, and how he worked out formulas. I'd seen the calculations: a smiley face plus a unicorn equaled a chainsaw, an apple and a penis equaled a heart. But I felt stupid for thinking the little man was my comrade and I left him shredding his bar napkin.

I decided to sit in the park above Bush Street. I knew Bell

would try to make me feel crazy. He rearranged his experience, cut out days and nights, tried to weld a nonlinear narrative. He told me once that he refused to be terrorized by time. He lied, forgot, wandered. He often told stories, like the one about meeting a trapeze artist in a bar, that I didn't think could be true. But then in the mail there would be an envelope with a circus insignia. He thought that when he left me I froze, and when he slipped back he set my life moving again, and the thing I hated most was that lately this was true.

I walked up California Street. It was lined with large Victorians, ornate as jewelry boxes. The houses were set back with small yards and as I passed one I saw two lovers in a slender alley. They were similarly dressed, with longish hair. One was standing behind the other so I couldn't tell if they were two men or two women or one of each. At first they seemed to be gazing at the moon, but then I saw their eyes were closed and I knew that one way or another they were making love.

THE PARK WAS AN OASIS AMONG THE STONE BUILDINGS AND asphalt of Nob Hill. It was arranged European-style with plots of calla lilies and fountains. There were benches with horny-toe-lizard legs and marble statues, one of young girls, bougainvillea grown over them. In the middle were reclining stone soldiers; their hard muscular demeanor reminded me of the leather monsters.

I sat in a far corner under a eucalyptus tree. The dye aroma had faded and the bourbon was just a warm sensation in my forehead. With my head in my hands, my features felt self-consciously delicate. But with my dyed hair I wasn't delicate. Now I resembled a certain kind of heartbreaking whore. She came to me: cheap handbag, lively hips and, linked to her, another picture—a makeshift suspension bridge swinging dangerously.

Bell wanted a disciple, someone who agreed that he was a new person, defining modern ways of living that had nothing to do with conventional commitment, someone capable of emotional toughness and moral vacuity. Sometimes I felt his ideas on relationships were brutal, more the outcome of a rough childhood and shaky adolescence than some inevitable futuristic truth. But other times there was a creeping anxiety that reminded me of Darwinism, made me wonder if I shouldn't listen if I wanted, as I did, to crush out the weak parts of myself.

Who was that little man? It would be easier if it were Kevin. Then there would be logical reasons for his growing preoccupation and moodiness. But his obsession with Kevin, his first love, was from a time ten years before, for a boy Bell admitted no longer existed. Sometimes I think I've fallen in love with Kevin along with other parts of Bell's past. What is love but a nostalgia for someone's history? Their boyhood haunts and sullen adolescence, their teenage trips cross-country and fights with their fathers and especially their old lovers? Sometimes I think I'm more interested in Bell's old lovers than I am in Bell. When I met him he was seeing a woman. And though I never said it, her description was enough like Marilyn's that I would think of her that way. Once I called her, the answering machine revealed a disembodied voice, low and secure, that made me feel stupid. But Bell only longs for Kevin, and sometimes, lately, I feel myself longing for him too.

Bell told me Kevin was dark with a tight hairless chest and a cock that was lipstick pink and slightly bowed to the left. He had intelligent eyes and a way of leaning toward you when he made a point. When I thought of Kevin he was surrounded with pale sunlight like Jesus. Sometimes he seemed to smile at me and I'd feel myself being pulled through my head into Bell's pearlish chain of memories. But once there, it was frustrating, like watching from the window as your beautiful young neighbors made love.

I thought of Bell yesterday, how he had satirized female cooing sounds, made his features dreamy, threw his head back in burlesque of a female orgasm. The mocking tone of his voice, "You take off that," when he stretched the material of the teddy then let the elastic edge snap against my skin. *He is bad for me.* This idea startled me and for a while I watched the fountain water splash between the figurines. A strong wind juggled the eucalyptus leaves. Nature is most beautiful in its movement: wind, water, the sinking sun. And it was just then that I saw a woman striding carelessly into the park.

She leaned on the edge of the fountain, letting her long hair brush the water, dressed in a paisley mini-dress and platform shoes. Wind rattled the lilies. She unbuckled her shoes and in one practiced movement pulled her dress over her head, and stepped into the fountain. I was startled, heard my breathing change like with sex. She was nude and so pale that the marble seemed sooty in comparison. When she looked my way her eyes caught light and burned red. If she saw me, she didn't seem to care. Her wide features were set smoothly, but it could just as easily have been the calm of the insane as true tranquillity. Quickly, she washed her feet, squatted, splashed water between her legs and over her breasts. Standing, she put her head between the thighs of a marble soldier and was encased for a moment in a pillar of foaming water. Sitting on the edge of the pool, she wrung her hair out and skimmed water from her body with flat open palms. There was a frail power about her, not dangerous, but resilient, as if she'd be hard to kill. I admired her absence of fear. The woman pulled on her dress, held her wet hair back as she strapped her platform shoes, then turned toward the milky lights of the Tenderloin.

I stood and watched her descent. The water seemed to absolve her. She held her shoulders regally and didn't look back, though I wanted her to turn and see me standing small against the trees. I felt better . . . maybe it was just that I knew Bell was meandering back to our apartment, past the Bacchus Kirk and the Malaysian bar on the corner. Or maybe the woman was a talisman, one that would help me in whatever came next.

OPENING THE APARTMENT DOOR, I THOUGHT THE LEOPARD'S lit eyes were two cigarette tips, but then felt the empty space and knew Bell was still not home. I didn't turn on the light. Whenever he left a place it was like he had never been there. I went around the room touching things. *This is his* . . . I was trying to get on intimate terms with the room. I needed it on my side.

Where would I be when he came in? On the bed would seem like I had already acquiesced. What if I leaned against the kitchen doorway and lit a cigarette? What would that say? Indifference? I could get into the tub, force him to talk to me through the closed door—I liked the implication of that—he would be confronted with the thought of my body, the image always more powerful than the actuality. And I wouldn't have to risk anything—I'd learned my lesson from the teddy. Or I could evoke my caustic mind by moving the straight-back chair into the middle of the room. I tried it but the chair looked like a stage prop and I hated myself for so carefully marking the power in each possibility.

I always thought of love as a stressful but productive state, because you wanted to improve yourself for your lover. But this was posing, not self-improvement. I wanted to be pleasing. That's what my mother did to try and keep my father. She looked pleasing, acted pleasing, made the house pleasing, all in an effort to mollify the uncertainties and unpleasantries of the unknown.

Right then the phone rang and I knew it was her. There's a telepathy between us sometimes so laserlike it frightens me. "Hi," she said. "How are you?"

My mother used her casual voice, one that hides a heightened desperation. I answered her usual inquiries. When we speak there is a suck that makes me lean into her voice; when I'm in her presence she gets a predatory look. My mother sees me as a part of her body, something that still belongs inside, a heart or a liver that she wants back.

"You remember the bank president? The one that had the affair with his secretary? It's been very messy, his wife won't give him a divorce. They say she's gone crazy. Yesterday, she walked into the bank and threw acid in the secretary's face." She stopped, not like the story was over, but like she was startled.

I examined the story for hidden meaning. While it could imply that my life also is in danger because I too dabble in perversity, it doesn't seem to fit the usual storyline of . . . me falling for a bad man like my father, or that even the wildest people eventually settle down. This one seemed on my side or Bell's . . . it was chaos.

She started to speak again, but I daydreamed. She was right, I didn't always listen, but it was her I was thinking of, remembering once, when I was four—I knew she was on a diet and I saw on TV something about an operation where you have part of your intestines removed to make you thinner and I told her about it, that she should have it. Her face got red, she was so angry that I felt confused, terrified, and trailed her the rest of the day trying to make it right. When I heard my father's tires on the gravel driveway I was sitting on the damp cellar stairs watching her put clothes into the washer. He walked down past me. She told him it had been a lousy day, she started to cry and said I had been rude to her. "I wasn't," I said, so upset I was light-headed. She looked at me directly for the first time since morning and said, "You want to cut me open."

The fabric of the memory dissolved and I heard her voice again. "How are you, honey? You know how I worry."

"I'm O.K.," I said, then lifted the phone away from my ear because I heard footsteps on the stairs. I told her quickly I had to go.

"O.K.," she said rigidly. No matter if we spoke for ten minutes or two hours she never wanted to hang up. "Bye now."

After our calls I always have an uneasy feeling. It's like that all the time with my mother. But I love her and probably most after a bad phone call: her fat upper arms, the way she talks like a baby when she's upset, those slippers with rosebuds she wears until the bottoms are flat and gray, and her sense of rigid honesty that has crippled her in this dishonest world.

Bell's steps were faint at first—then firmer, centered and serious, paced like a showdown. I ran to the kitchen, realized while he searched for his keys that it was silly for me to hide, so I swung the refrigerator door open knowing the white light would be far off and eerie in the apartment. The key was in the lock . . . there were several odd tinfoil shapes, a green pitcher of orange juice, a single jar of shrimp cocktail, a bit of browning smoked salmon and half a tomato that was losing muscle tone. The problem with being a modern woman, I thought, as the front door swung wide, is that you have to pretend to be stronger than you are.

He walked straight to me and leaned against the doorway. His hair was scruffy and his face showed stubble. His cigarette had a long ash which he knocked into his hand. He drew, the tip glowed, underlighting his face. Like a good actor,

Bell's demeanor was different now than in the bar. His presence made the air in the apartment thicker. I turned on the faucet. The water beat into the sink. I drank down a full glass, then poured another. My proximity to his body made me feel unsure. Maybe I overreacted. The faucet surged. I knew when I turned it off I'd have to say something. His usual approach would be to either act more wronged than me or, by being extreme—"Do you want me to stay chained to the bed?"—make me seem unreasonable.

He would make me speak first, it was always his way. He knew silence was a reprimand, as disturbing as vomit, and in near hysteria I'd rush to fill it, clean the room, make it comfortable. I noticed the skin around his eyes was thin and gray, maybe he was exhausted, but it made him look unhinged and I always associated eyes like that with evil. I realized how my thoughts, since he'd been gone, made him a stranger to me.

"Where have you been?" I hadn't meant to start off like that, I knew it would be better to seem indifferent.

He let one hip loosen, sloshed into contrapposto and slanted his eyes. Bell probably meant to look sexy or powerful, but instead he seemed dipped in sleaze.

"On the way to get cigarettes I got lost, ended up wandering as far as Bernal Heights. There is a lovely park where homeless men cook over sterno ovens and a little old man plays his fiddle on a park bench." He meant to sound cute, to try to evaporate tension and show that I was being possessive and martyrish. When I didn't respond he tried again. "I like your hair." He leaned forward, tried to touch me.

I swung my head back, bumped it hard on the cabinet. "You fucker, I was worried you were dead."

His face drew up, mouth tightened. "Bullshit. You thought I was screwing someone. If you were completely confident in me, you wouldn't even be interested. You need a love triangle, Jesse, to make you feel alive."

I was addicted to the fear of infidelity and I believed relationships were like the trinity: there were the two human participants, one always more godlike than the other, and then there was the thing between them, the other—an aberrant philosophy, a person or a phantom like Kevin.

"I don't care what you do," I lied and he smirked to show he recognized it as one. "But you can't just wander off."

"I couldn't do it, if I wasn't sure you were here," he said.

"Tough luck," I said. He was trying to conjure up the Noble Wife. I should be proud to suffer for him. I tried to brush past him, but he grabbed my arm and said, "I need you with me."

There was a rusty quality to his voice that implied insecurity. Bell was like this. His posturing was a sign that inside he felt tender and helpless. There were times when he asked my advice on gifts for his family, or if I thought he'd said the wrong thing at a dinner party. It reminded me of him detached from his bad behavior, how I loved him and didn't really want to leave at all. I decided not to be mean, but honest. "I'm sick of you thinking you have the right to wander off."

"I thought you were the kind to allow me my mental infidelities."

It was going to become a discourse on abstract freedom, he would go through his haggard points: about the individual, about how poor people think they're free because they could leave the country, could go to college or win the lottery. But it seldom happened, instead they worked like prisoners and lived in apartments barely more comfortable then cells. All he wanted, he claimed, was this—he needed to dream.

He was staring coldly at his veiny hand. Twisting his cigarette butt in our blue glass ashtray. While his head was ducked I saw his crucifix over the sink: a pale purple Jesus on a cross so white it glowed.

"It makes me feel horrible how you moon over Kevin," I said slowly. He flinched at Kevin's name, and walked to the couch, sat sloppily, kicked at a penny on the floor. "My life was very pleasant when I knew Kevin."

"Everyone's life is pleasant at seventeen."

"It was more than that. Everything was new, now I'm like a junkie, I seem to need more severe doses of experience to feel anything."

In all our arguments I wanted him to deface Kevin's memory, to say it had been perverse or that he was emotionally undeveloped, that he preferred women, that he preferred me to Kevin.

Bell was quiet. There were always these moments he receded, felt soulfully misunderstood, above domestic conflict, sullied by interaction with anyone. He crossed his legs, his gaze following the jagged tops of buildings up the hill. He was too beautiful for this world.

I told him he was the devil. I'd said this often and fondly, but now I said it again, burlesquing the way I used to. "You are the devil. I should have left you in the beginning when I saw you dancing with that black boy, putting streamers around his neck, letting him sit on your lap."

A flush spidered into Bell's cheeks. "The minister's daughter speaks."

Once he started insisting I was prudish, moralistic, crippled by my father, there was no use arguing. He slipped into his extremist mode, called me bourgeois, claiming he was a proletarian, ridiculed my classical education, said he was a student of the streets.

"Look," he continued. "Everyone would align with the devil if they could."

"And then they'll drop the bomb."

Several seconds passed before he said with perfect dramatic timing, "Pleasure, my dear, does not always equal sin."

When cornered I sounded wifish and conventional. I was silent.

He was getting agitated, rocking himself on the couch, he spoke with force. "Admit that either of us could go to a bar, pick up a stranger and have better sex with them than we could with each other."

"That's because when you're in love your problems follow you into bed."

"You've told me yourself, you fantasize about strangers, about giving pleasure to several men at once." He looked me right in the eyes, stood slowly, puffed up, trying to make his point with his body.

"I told you because I thought you would understand. It's like thinking about murdering someone versus doing it."

He took my hand, held it palm up, rubbed his fingertips over my lifeline so it tickled. "Just imagine if I were a stranger, if I saw you on the street, noticed you because your hair covered one side of your face and your hips moved in a lazy way that said fuck me." He put his loose hand above the first one and pulled me toward him slowly as if my arm were a rope. I could feel his breath on my face. "I'd follow you down the street to the steps of your building. Watch your slender thighs beneath your dress disappearing behind the door, thinking how wet you might be, how your breasts would be full and cool to touch. Then I'd follow you up the stairs. The door would open. In the slant of light from the hallway I'd see you nude on the bed."

He pulled me to him, grabbed a side of my ass in each hand and whispered into my ear. "I'd sit first on the chair near the bed and touch you, trace your neck bones, my fingers rounding your breasts in tiny spirals until I got to the nipple. Then I'd bow my head and suck."

My face pressed into his hair; smoke, eucalyptus. I could feel myself getting wet and I knew I wouldn't try to stop him. Even though this was not what I wanted, it was a semblance of it. I convinced myself that him wanting sex meant he wanted me, but it seemed naive and overly hopeful, like a schoolgirl or a dreamy whore.

"I want to fuck," Bell said, dramatically. Like everything in bed, you pretend; pretend you are inarticulate, more animal, more powerful or weaker than you are. I was flattered he would put this energy into seduction and I allowed him to maneuver me through the room then trip me down onto the bed.

The blinds were up and the tall buildings zoomed high. He moved his tongue over my eyes and into my ears. I put my hands inside his pants, the hair there was moist and his cock was stretched smooth. Bell pulled my shirt up over my head so I couldn't see. I felt his hand working my bra clasp. Would he leave me like this? I raised my arms and he pulled the shirt off, lapped at my nipples until they stood up hard like nuts. Bell rested his head on my stomach and unlatched my pants. His fingers gentle inside the folds of wet skin. I wiggled my jeans down, getting only one leg free before Bell stopped me, spread my legs, kneeled down between them, put his hands under my ass and lifted up my sex as if he was filling his hands with water to drink.

I felt the bed fall away, and the floor, and the ceiling and the walls, and I had the sensation we were floating out the window. Time lifted too and left us, because when you're fucking it is impossible to think of the next ten minutes or the next ten years. Because fucking, when it's good, seems like everything and there is pain in the pleasure when you remember things that are horrible, until you are hardly alive, and so many times good things turn bad that you decide to live the life you fear most, the ordinary one, the one that is easy and hard. But now I think of the other time he made me stand on the chair and pulled down my tights, the way I saw his fingers disappearing inside me. But I don't want to be a lover like this so my days are spent wandering, phantoms of a tongue, a cock or a finger flaring under my eyelids.

By the way he braced himself, sheets clenched in his fists, and how he tucked his pelvis, tried instinctively for an angle that would put his sperm closer to my cervix I knew he was close. I thought of what I always do . . . putting my ass high, having someone come between my breasts. Then the usual chant to push me over . . . marry me, fuck me, marry me, fuck me, marry me, fuck me. I had a momentary thought that we were feeding on each other. His cock pulsed and there was the sensation of water rising quickly, like in a flood and suddenly I was deaf and dumb with pleasure. He fell on top of me. His chest trapped air, made a sound like a horn. It was a rule between us that we never spoke afterward. He was on the side of gesture, not of words, and accused me of ruining moments by defining them.

He slipped out, rolled over. His breath loosened and I could tell that he was falling asleep. Bell became that precious thing: the sublime sleeping child. What if I didn't need to recognize all the extra static of our relationships? Maybe everything was OK, at least for now.

For a long time I couldn't sleep. I was too conscious of the different textures of the sheet and the pillowcase, the air and the sharp slants of light. The walls, too, with their grainy malevolent shapes. I felt frightened, snuggled back into the cave of Bell's chest. This is the one I've chosen. He makes meaning for me. Not by doing anything particular, but in the way he speaks and moves and how he sleeps abandonedly beside me. Quickly then my mind slipped into dislogic and I saw a random pattern of floating objects: Bell's slender fingers, my mother's face, the deflated dye bottle, the woman in the fountain. These strung together like charms on a bracelet and I let them lead me into a silky unconsciousness and then finally into sleep.

Chapter

Two

IN THE SILENCE OF THE BART TRAIN ON THE WAY TO MADAM Pig's, I could only think of last night: how we slept curled close like petals, how at dawn Bell woke to tell me his dream—we were in a driverless taxi following a tennis ball I'd hit hard enough that it still soared above us. We chased the ball down a road surrounded with abandoned factories and tin warehouses, then made a violent turn into a subdivision of burnt-out ranch houses. The last thing he remembered was squatting at the foot of a dolmen of seared wood, the bloodied light at the horizon.

At first I thought the dream seemed a good omen, maybe even a mark of my power. But any contentment with last night wore off like the fading charm of a hit song. I realized the bombed suburbia was his idea of domesticity in general and our future specifically.

It seemed crazy that I stayed. Bell made me feel edgy and hysterical, but at least this way I was alive. Also, I suspected I was close to winning him and if I did he would become a docile and genial lover. But the myth of breaking a man was stupid, just as stupid as believing there would be any long-term good in the sexual ending we tumbled into last night.

The BART swayed toward Oakland. I thought love was about forgetting yourself, a sensation that calmed and centered you, like being pleasantly stoned, but all I felt was a speedy panic. I couldn't forget myself for one minute and it was disconcerting how Bell's life seemed superimposed over mine. Even now, Bell would be sitting at the table by the window smoking a cigarette, watching traffic, glancing occasionally at the play script he was to audition for today. He'd be drinking tea with a splash of bourbon to settle his nerves. But it seemed like my own hand poised on the teacup, my own ear listening to the water rattle into the tub for his bath.

Bell was exotic to me still. If I could learn to think of him as a normal person I could disentangle myself. I had never known anyone like him or seen a life like his. He took me to the velvety apartment of an actress who had a dozen fur coats and a voice that sounded like gin and cigarettes. When we went to the museum in Golden Gate Park Bell stared at the Caravaggio for twenty minutes. I loved how he was always on the side of life's losers and considered them more intuitive and intelligent than others. He wore secondhand suits and read obscure books in Greek. The slender volumes lay elegantly as tulips around the apartment. And when I looked inside, the indecipherable alpha-

bet seemed like the language of dreams. After my bland suburban past this was as powerful as heroin.

From the elevated track I saw the front of the train curve
ahead. Behind it, huge Trojan horses unloaded steel barrels
from ocean tankers, and refinery stacks blasted blue fire. A
police helicopter hovered. At the sharpest point of the curve I
thought, *This is how things are beautiful now.* There were
aluminum warehouses in dull shades of gray and green and,
nearer the track, boarded-up houses.

The BART slid into one station after another. Maybe I
had ruined my life. Everything you do matters too much and it's
possible to poison your present relationship by actions made in
the past. With Bell, it was his obsession with Kevin. I watched
my own past work adversely on lovers, when I admitted juggling
men and lying to them. Infidelity is a tricky business. There's
less meaning in an infidelity than in a relationship, so I would
lie to Bell. And though I wasn't now, the fact that I would lie
might mean he was lying.

I wondered how Madam Pig would be feeling today? Pig
was a huge woman who wore tent dresses with sparkly thread
and patterns of tropical birds. Her hair was dyed strawberry
blond and her face was always covered with a generous amount
of make-up. She had long fingernails, always perfectly mani-
cured and painted a shade of pink she said reminded her of
Persia. Her name came from a story about her ex-husband
having a pet pig that could smoke cigars and drink cans of beer.
Pig was the best storyteller I'd ever encountered, specializing in
adultery tales where women, hearing their husbands unexpect-

edly on the stairs, make their lovers hide naked on the fire escape.

There were lots of rumors about how she came into money. She said it was left to her by a contessa she once accompanied on a trip through the Middle East. Others said it was her husband's money, that he'd been heir to a jelly business in Wales, that he paid her off to live with a Parisian starlet. One woman told me Pig strangled him, buried him in the empty lot beside the house. People said she'd starred in blue movies, that she had been the madam of the most stylish bordello in New Orleans.

Wherever the money came from, she didn't mind spending it. Pig loved having parties with giant lasagnas and champagne fountains. She lit candles and let the drag queens fight over the record player. I met several people there: a feminist trying to destroy the myth of the aesthetic canon, musicians who insisted house music was the blues of the nineties and a performance artist who covered himself with animal blood and said narrative was dead.

At the last party, I was in the kitchen helping Pig prepare an appetizer of avocado halves with cheese and shrimp when she turned to me, held her glass out for more wine and said, "Bell's beautiful, isn't he?" I didn't answer. "But couldn't you marry someone else and take him as a lover?"

I was so startled I spilled burgundy over her fingers, tried clumsily to defend myself, saying I didn't want to get married, that I appreciated his spontaneity. She stood back from the oven, her face flushed and eyes a little teary from the heat and

took my hands, looked at me as my mother might. "Well
. . . I've never known a beautiful girl who wasn't doomed."

Later that night, after two young Irishmen sang a Celtic
song about a ship full of sheep sinking into the sea, Pig stood
woozily, holding her glass high, and began to toast. It was late,
everyone lying languidly over the furniture. "To love," she said,
"that delicate egg . . . and to evil . . . which teases and tempts
us as a good lover might." Pig moved her head with great
drama. "Also, to my dear departed husband . . . who was lovely
to see with a day's beard stubble." The drag queens giggled.
"And most of all, to the mental and physical wasteland of the
future. Finally our inner boredom and bareness will not be
intimidated by a lush and healthy nature."

There were scattered claps all around and Madam Pig
blushed, turned toward the stereo. She wanted to hear the
Hildegard Knef record. But before she took a single step, Pig
swayed slightly, raised her hand up as if grabbing for a butterfly,
then fell to her knees and rolled onto the floor.

For a moment, she lay still, then said, her face pressed
into the carpet, "Could someone please take me to my room?"

Three men rushed up, took her legs and shoulders,
heaved her massive body up like it was a pool table. I cradled her
head, which was limp as a baby's. On the way she spoke incoher-
ently, told the men she loved them, said we could all come and
live with her. Drool ran down Pig's cheek and onto my hand.
They laid her gently on the bed, stood awkwardly, instinctively
folding their hands like in church. The oldest one gestured with
his head that they should leave. He squeezed her hand and her

eyes opened, she said, "Let them dance." I threw a blanket over her, closed the drapes against the faint orange industrial light. She asked me in a blurry voice to come over three times a week, that she needed me now and would pay me well, because she suspected very soon she would die.

The BART stopped high above the street. Walking down the steps past the cement columns, I saw, lying in the tall weeds, two lovers pressed close, old newspapers and fast-food containers scattered all around them. The girl's hair was long, stretched out like ivy. They didn't notice me. The noise from the highway and the BART passing created a kind of negative silence around them.

This part of Oakland was barren compared to the civilized patter of San Francisco, even anemic with its tin buildings and fenced lots. In front of the station was a supermarket that sold grapes for thirty cents a pound, a variety of peppers, prickly pears and other Mexican products. Behind the market stood a row of pasty houses with dirt yards. There were empty crack vials all over the sidewalk and a dead cat in a cardboard box near the dumpster.

A man in a white Ford by the pay phones kept saying, "Hey, skinny. Hey, skinny." I scanned him quickly. He wore a Caribbean shirt open to show his chest hairs and a slender gold chain. He whistled, but I still wouldn't turn. "Your pussy stinks," he said as I walked away. "I can smell it from here." He laughed like he really thought he was funny. I hurried past his headlights with decals of Jesus, past a wall of graffiti tags and a silent brick factory. Through empty window frames I could see figures sitting on mattresses spread over the floor.

Pig's house was covered with vines. Hers was a stone Victorian, impressive still with the cherubic faces on every cornice. The gutter loosened and slumped, jammed now with the sharp leaves of the lemon tree. Paint chips blew off like snow in every wind. And the flower boxes of silk irises had paled in the rain. Every other house on her street had been demolished, the earth turned over, the ground pockmarked with deep filthy puddles. Beyond the mud, the houses were boarded up, adjacent lots filled with trash and sofas swollen with rats. The path to the door was marked with chunks of slate. Burrs stuck to my pants as I passed. Inside I paused to rest, picking off the burrs, letting my eyes adjust to the cooler dark air. On one side, the dining room, which always had a scent of rose petals and chamomile tea. Here was a long walnut table and strange paintings of stylized factory workers in a maze of equipment and smoke. Madam Pig had her garnet glass collection displayed, hundreds of red plates, mugs, goblets, salt shakers, candle holders, gravy dishes and ashtrays. With the curtains drawn they seemed demure. But on the nights Pig lit her candles, the glass sent candied light every which way. The living room door was shut, but I could hear the grandfather clock behind the velvet couch.

"Is that you, Jesse?" Madam Pig yelled from the kitchen.

"It's me!" I answered, walking the hall toward her voice. Along the wall hung pastel portraits of Madam Pig's only child, Madison. The girl had shell-white skin and blond hair. It might be her paleness or that there were ten portraits on each side, but they always seemed to glow and animate like a film clip.

Pig sat at the round table in the kitchen eating cold raspberry soup from a bowl and drinking red wine. She looked well today, but with her bulldog face and strange red shade of bouffant hair, she was always a spectacle. Since Pig never left the house I knew her flush could not be from exercise, but a particularly lucky application of make-up. Today her eyebrows were superbly drawn.

"I love cold soup. It goes so well on these days when I'm the last person in the world." Pig stared into her soup as if something she lost years ago would surface any minute.

"Soup's good," I said, never knowing if her exclamatory statements were meant to be answered.

She looked up. "Jesse," she said quickly, "did you bring some mangoes?"

I shook my head. "But I can go look for some." Pig looked at me like I was crazy, her eyes wide. "Why would you want to go out there?" She gestured to the window and the mud lot.

"I meant I'd go to the store to look." It was always hard for me to know what to say to Pig. Besides, whatever I answered never seemed to pertain to her reply. "No," she muttered, "no, no, no . . ."

I sat in an overstuffed chair. I loved this room. The wallpaper, a big bawdy pattern of magnolias drenched in hazy moonlight. Pig sat across from me at the round cherry table with mismatched chairs. At first I thought the upholstered chairs looked strange in the kitchen, until I realized the house's inner logic of abundance and how silly Madam Pig would look in a spindly chair.

I watched her elegantly spoon the soup into her mouth and flip the pages of an old magazine; there were stacks all over the table. She read them, some even twenty-five years old, like it was new information.

"You look well," I said.

At this she raised her head, gave me a look that showed her disapproval of innocuous pleasantries, plunked her spoon into the bowl and said suspiciously, "Who told you that you have to do what you don't want?" I could tell by the set of her chin that she had been thinking of this all weekend. "Your mother?" Pig asked. "It's a shame what mothers do. What they really mean is that women get stronger by the bad things that happen to them. Not that you have to make bad things happen to you, and more importantly, pretend to like situations that you don't."

The last phrase made my eyes well, and Madam Pig said, "Oh honey, did he leave you again?"

I nodded my head and wiped my eyes, staring at the glass bowl filled with oranges in the table's center. I told Pig how he had gone to get cigarettes and not come home all night. Then how I searched for him and spied while he had spoken with the little man.

She interrupted me to say thoughtfully that she didn't

hate her former husband, "I only wish he never again treats anyone like a cow." She had a vacant look then, like she had to go inside and think of what she said.

I felt uncomfortable in the silence and stared at her magazine, one picture of an astronaut floating unconnected to surface or spaceship—he seemed threatening with the black mask of his helmet twinkling.

When she saw me staring she said, "It's amazing what you can learn from watching someone."

"I don't know that I learned anything from watching Bell."

"Once you see your lover doing something you could never discuss with him then sooner or later you will leave."

I thought how once at a bar Bell was mesmerized by a pair of drag queens in their long black wigs, go-go boots and miniskirts.

"Can't you just start up with someone else?" she asked sympathetically. "Oh I know I'm always rallying for it, but adultery is so much better when you have an ax to grind."

I said, "Bell is the one I have chosen," and the sound of my voice frightened me. It was firm and inarguable like a born-again Christian.

Pig pushed her soup dish back. "Well," she said, "there is nothing I can do if you won't listen to reason. But I do want to tell you one story. It happened to an old friend of mine. She was a conservative woman, but lovely with kitty-cat blue eyes and peanut-butter-colored hair. She was queen of the flower festival and decided at twenty, though she had her choice of many, to marry a minister. He told her that they would do good works and always have a hundred dollars in their pockets. Sometimes when they were alone she sensed something cruel in his profile, something soft and perverse around his mouth. But they married anyway, had several good years, then a slew of horrible ones. She got fat like me and started to act mean and arrogant and before she knew it he had the smell of other women on him and when she reached for him in bed he'd say, 'Don't embarrass yourself.' "

I felt my eyes get warm and milky. "That's my mother's story," I said to Pig. "I told you that."

"Oh," she said, "no wonder in my mind it seemed to pertain to you." She didn't look at me. Her cheeks got pink under the heavy spots of rouge. She rose awkwardly, her grand body shivering, shifting like a yacht pulling out of dock.

"Time for my bath," she said.

IN THE LAUNDRY ROOM OFF THE KITCHEN THE WASHER WAS A slick erotic white. I loaded Pig's colossal slips and bras into the washing machine. Upstairs the water was still beating into the tub. I could hear the sloshing and squeezy echo of Pig settling in, her thighs relaxing heavily against the sides, her back sinking low against the porcelain. Pig's underwear, all in pastel colors and the size of office trash bags, reminded me of the style I wore in grade school. Why did fat embarrass me? Fat people couldn't hide their weakness or sorrow like most could. I used to wake at night and pull a pillow to my stomach, worrying about getting fat. But as I loaded the washer with her oversized dresses, Pig didn't seem tragic but abundant. I almost felt a comfort in her hugeness.

In the kitchen I poured dish soap into a sponge and washed the green ice-tea glasses and started on the flowered soup tureen filmed with hardened raspberries. Because of Bell and my parents I sometimes felt undermined, then other times I thought I was better off because I had gotten over a certain sentimental view of the world. I brooded on this as I ripped up several pairs of ancient boxers in order to dust, then carried the cloth fragments of a polka-dot pair to the living room. I liked dusting . . . there wasn't the strenuous arm movement of other household chores, but a kind of elegant glide that even the smartest lady would be willing to do. You could imagine Virginia Woolf dusting, but to envision her cleaning a toilet was impossible. The white couch, the clock on the mantle, the lamp with the porcelain stem; this room was not as eclectic as the others. Instead each object was like a museum piece, icy with purpose. They were like the memories that interacted or repelled to create my changing moods.

Pig called out. I stood still, worried she had slipped on the tiles, lost her breath, realized her heart was about to explode, but then her voice straightened and I heard that she was calling for more wine.

MADAM PIG'S WINE GLASS SAT ON THE TUB'S LEDGE. THE STEAM thinned and her muddy features took on definition. Except for her lyrical personality, it was hard to believe she had ever been beautiful.

"Would you wash my back and make the symbols like you do," she asked. "Don't deny it. I've felt them: stop signs, peace signs, Z's. It feels so good to absorb information through the skin."

Her body underwater was gelatinous and rosy as a Rubens. If you didn't know what a body was supposed to look like, Madam Pig's body would be like a sloppy dream. Her breasts were buoyant and her ancient nipples bobbed at the surface. No matter how many times I saw her naked I was always surprised and a little horrified. But the philosophy of the tub, a woman and her bath, was different than the bedroom—there should be no taint of male criteria.

She spoke lazily about her aches and pains and eventually her voice mellowed into self-conscious wisdom. "When I was your age, Jesse, I'd see some gesture, like the way a strange man opened his jacket or how a girl lifted her foot to check her heel, and I wouldn't be able to lace it into my memory. Instead, the image would be stilled, it would have the awful inactivity of death and this magnified the moment around me: my heart, car tremors, clouds, people working their bodies. Very plainly then I'd see the dark silence of the end. But now that I know death is near, it's not dramatic or startling, just boring."

"You wouldn't die," I said, "if you went to the doctor." She ignored me, pretended to wash her elbow. Her pubic hair reminded me of some elaborate seaweed.

"Why don't you call your daughter?" I asked.

"I haven't seen Madison for five years," Pig said.

"So, you could call her up now."

"I was hoping you would call her."

"I don't even know her."

Pig closed her eyes so long I thought she had fallen asleep. "In an effort," Pig said, "to explain why I can never call her I will tell you how Madison came to leave. Steven left me. He had a private income and those people never really get attached to anything. Madison took it hard, stayed in her room, cut her hair short and got a nose ring. And in the same spirit she bought a wolf. It was half grown and very tame, a charcoal-and-honey colored animal with dark green eyes. She named it London and fed it hamburgers, sometimes the occasional black-market squirrel. We kept it tied in the back. So many times it pulled its stake out we finally got a boy to pour a cement base. It barked a lot and whined. The neighborhood kids threw sticks over the fence to tease it. They thought it was a rabid dog. After a while Madison started asking if we could set it free in Big Sur. I was in a sick mood and liked to watch the thing suffer. Madison began threatening to leave, but I didn't believe her. One morning I woke before dawn to a horrible yelping in the backyard. The air felt like certain Good Fridays. The wolf's chain was pulled tightly over the fence. I looked through the wood planks and saw the wolf's dead eyes and Madison's smiling face. She had called the wolf, who then tried to jump the fence in an effort to follow her." Pig looked into the water. "It hung itself as Madison watched . . . What kind of a girl would do a thing like that?" she asked solemnly. The lilac soap slipped into the

42

water. The plop disturbed her and she continued. "I haven't seen her since. I heard she was working in the Tenderloin and I had a detective follow her. Get the brass box." I brought it over and she opened it and handed a slip of paper to me. "Go to her. Tell her I'm dying."

"Why don't you go?"

"You know I never leave the house."

I looked at the address, then at Pig. Though she looked drained, the story seemed false. But I felt sorry for her, and her expectant face reminded me of my mother's; both had the cast of women that have been left in middle age. As she pulled herself out with a great suck of water, I handed her a towel.

"I hate the vague egalitarianism of these times, it insists that there are no qualitative standards. Judge and be judged," Pig said. "That is my saying."

She wrapped the towel around her head like a turban and I helped with her robe. Her face was red from the bath. At the banister, Pig had to stop because she felt dizzy. She tipped way forward and I realized then, because of the hingey way her head bobbed, that she was very drunk. Pig's head dropped lower. She gagged and a long line of glittering burgundy ribboned down the stairwell. Lifting her head sleepily, she said, "I want you to find her." I wiped her mouth and helped her down the hall to her room.

The green curtains were shut and the single candle looked fuzzy, like a dandelion. It was mid-afternoon, though inside the room it always seemed like midnight. She clutched my arm and asked if I'd get her a cardboard box from the bookshelf.

Inside were photographs, large black-and-whites on thin paper: Pig's husband leaning against the door of his race car. He wore sunglasses and there was something in the firm set of his mouth that told me Pig had had a very hard time. There were others, a lovely woman, who I figured was his sister, in a blouse with a Peter Pan collar, her dark hair tied back with a scarf.

"Who's that?" I asked.

Pig did not open her eyes, did not answer.

"You were beautiful," I said, feeling embarrassed. I shuffled the photos together and handed them to her.

"I was." She grabbed my wrist hard. "You don't want to end up like me."

I wanted to yell at Pig that there was no more poignancy in the aging of a beautiful woman than a plain one. If beautiful girls had higher expectations it was only because of vanity, not that they were better people or more blessed. And besides, it didn't seem possible I could end up like Pig. She let her nails dig into the soft part of my arm and with the pain I thought, *Once she was like me.*

She must have noticed my look of recognition because she released me and I walked over to the window, held the curtain back. There was a milky lavender rising beyond the power lines.

"You can go now," she said softly. "I'll be all right."

I blew out the candle and walked to the door. Pig sat up into the crack of hall light.

"Remember, Jesse," she said, "there is no black angel but love."

44

Chapter

Three

Outside the market street bart station, pavement puddles reflected bits of clouds, pigeons balanced on the Woolworth's sign and punks panhandled the tourists in line for the cable cars. Across the street an abandoned porno theater still showed posters of women in garters and push-up bras. The prospect of a search gave the streets a tingly importance. I decided to go see Bell at the costume shop he worked at on Eddy. As I passed the Golden Nugget on the corner, drinkers raised their heads, men and women who looked alike, as if booze had an androgynous physical ideal.

The shop was called Ozymandias. There was a Jesus costume in the window complete with stigmata paste-ons and a crown of thorns. Waiting to cross the street I picked out Bell moving among the carrels of magic tricks, the familiar motion of him pulling his jacket up over his stooped shoulders. The owner, a tiny unsmiling man in a baseball cap, dead-bolted the door behind them.

Bell turned up Jones and I realized he was walking toward the theater for his audition. I followed. He didn't seem particularly nervous or troubled, though on Sutter and Jones he stopped for a moment, sunk his hands into his pockets, leaned back against a brick wall and looked up into the sky. His leisurely motions reminded me of dreams . . . watching your lover speak in hushed tones with someone else. Bell put his flattened hand against his chest. Could he be thinking of the morning his father died? How he had woken from a one-night stand in a strange house, in a neighborhood he didn't recognize, how he walked to the nearest bus stop and shyly asked the driver how to get home? Maybe he was thinking of how Kevin would drift into a café with an atlas under his arm and order a glass of red wine? How his nostalgic yearning for his teenage lover was about to be derailed by a heterosexual reality: Kevin's marriage.

I FOLLOWED HIM, AT A SAFE DISTANCE, INTO THE THEATER AND sat in the back row. It was a small place with abodons and other dark angels smiling down from the cornices. The stage was lit for a moody dream sequence, so dim it took a minute to see the green couch, the kitchen table and the single wooden folding chair.

People were scattered in the front rows where Bell had already taken a place. To one side an older man with a thick waist held a clipboard. Beside him stood a very thin woman in jeans. Their heads were ducked in consultation. The woman shrugged her shoulders, put her hand on her hip and lit a cigarette. Blue smoke rose above her short brown hair. The man called a name and a stocky young man rose and headed for the stage.

"You got it? Your wife is sleeping around," she said. "And forget your lines. We're looking for something fresh."

He didn't look old enough to have a wife and I could tell by the way he took the stage that he was uncomfortable. His face compressed with seriousness. He sat stiffly on the couch like it belonged in his old aunt's parlor. After a minute he jumped up and began to pace.

"You dirty cow." His words echoed. "If I had a gun I'd shoot you. You're like a myna bird, you see something pretty and you just pick it up," he ranted. Even from where I sat I saw his face was red. "It's not that you're fucking someone else, it's that you've had someone else's cock and didn't give me a chance to decide whether I wanted mine there, too." He went back to the couch, sat back, crossed his arms over his chest and said, as if to himself and more slowly, "God knows I could never touch you now."

I was moved by his naive delivery, his seriousness. Maybe he reminded me of my first lover? I could be kind to him, like a lover on a one-night stand, because I knew he didn't have a chance. He went over to the woman and she patted him on the back, speaking to him in an insider's whisper.

I remembered again why I hated theater: the melodramatic idea that a person could wake up over toast or driving to the gynecologist and see they'd ruined their life. And I don't like feeling responsible for humans on stage. It reminded me, with its confrontational emotionality, of the homeless men on the street who told you their sad life stories, then asked for change.

She must have admitted he wasn't right for the part because he grabbed his raincoat from the backseat and walked noisily past me, out the door. The man and woman spoke together softly, until the others waiting began to grumble. From his clipboard the man called Bell.

"Same thing," he said. Bell nodded, walked toward the stage. He hadn't worked much since I'd known him, so it was odd to watch his attempt at professional composure. In our own conversations there were moments he would perform, his turn of phrase or the graceful way he raised his glass.

To watch him reminded me of my photographs, snapshots of shirtless boys in the Mission and Mexican girls in first communion dresses. I quit because they seemed voyeuristic. I started thinking in terms of the single frame. My brain felt dry, lacking the fluid it takes to link images into confluence. I think of going back to photography sometimes because people become intimate when you have a camera. Everyone has one expression that they believe is attractive or profound. Faces reveal a frightening self-deception.

Bell sat on the chair by the table, which strangely resembled the black table at home, hands folded in his lap, his face set toward the seats. It took me a minute to realize he was pretending. He let his shoulders fall slightly and was quiet so long one man coughed and another let out a long fed-up sigh. Without changing his expression, Bell said, "You should have told me, Jesse." The stage light became as hazy as a million suns.

"Not that I didn't suspect it, coming home late with your legs clamped and the nape of your neck smelling like whiskey." He stood and walked over to the couch. Even from where I sat I could see him snarl. "But it doesn't matter if you're fucking Kevin as long as you know now I will too."

His voice continued, but I didn't hear anything. My head was full; sloshing water, heat spots, beating wings. I felt sick and fumbled out of my seat. The raw street light was brutal, so I stepped into a Moroccan deli, stared at the tubed meats, the squares of cheese in wedding-dress shades. It wasn't that he had used my name or mixed it up with Kevin's, but that I would never know whether Bell was acting or not.

MADISON WORKED AT A BAR CALLED CARMEN'S SNUGGLED BE-tween the Fallen Angel and a brightly lit Chinese cafeteria. The block was mostly boarded-up storefronts. But there were a few older pubs designated by the San Francisco symbol for bar, a pink neon martini glass. Across the street was a massage parlor called the China Girl. I wandered into the Lusty Lady, a few doors down, hoping to calm myself a little before I approached Madison.

Inside, I saw a row of numbered doors and disks of refracted light from the glass ball in the foyer. A Japanese woman in high heels replaced my dollars with pentagon-shaped coins, nude girls on either side. The booth reeked of cleaning fluid, and disco music pounded through the wall. I slipped a token into its slot and a panel rose like a suburban garage door. Behind the plastic window, a forty-year-old woman danced in an otherwise empty room. Empty, I thought, so men could unobstructedly ease the woman into memory, take her home and into bed. As the door opened, her feet were revealed first. She seemed huge, big-boned with shaggy hair dyed black, more vulgar than sexy. She had a bored, tattered look that reminded me of a zoo animal. The woman that serviced the other angle was younger and slender with a pixie cut. They never talked or looked at the leering men in the windows as they swung their butts and opened their pelvises. I felt a tightening between my legs. Did I want the woman that rubbed her nipples and grabbed her crotch or was my desire elicited by the massive lust emanating from the other booths? I left quickly wondering if being wanted so intensely could make a woman feel strong.

Down the block, in Carmen's storefront window, a TV on a Doric column showed the horizontal chaos of static. Inside, the walls were sheet metal. Reflected shards of purple light gave the bartender's silver eye make-up and angular hairdo a futuristic glow. The waitresses wore see-through tops and glitter in their hair. Computerized devices sent out bands of fractured light like the flames glowing around a sacred heart. Black lights illuminated the white collars and cuffs of the businessmen gathered at the bar. Carmen's wasn't worn and melancholy like the Black Rose, but brutal and energized like an operating room. A

hundred TVs covered the walls, showing continuous car-crash
footage—splatters of glass, a panicked eye, puddling blood.

People slowly packed in, squat rockers with skull rings
and men in blue pants with the musty smell of work. There were
a couple of skinheads in boots and flight jackets, their skulls
buffed up to an evil gleam. And scattered women: full-time
drinkers with bland sheepish faces and pale rocker chicks with
black lipstick and deep circles under their eyes. Everyone looked
uncomfortable and eyed each other suspiciously.

I ordered a vodka, thinking of it as a companion, wondering if Bell had passed his audition and if the women in the
Lusty Lady enjoyed their work. The music was distracting. The
beat doubled my heart's and the melodies were woven with
sirens and sound bytes of political speeches. I couldn't think
coherently, but that was O.K. because I wanted to quit process-
ing. I wanted to try and let things build up around me, encase
me like an exoskeleton.

The music changed abruptly to an Indian sitar, and a test
tube of green light appeared on the elevated stage. A woman
rose from beneath through a trapdoor, dancing languidly toward the light, testing it as if it were water, first a pinkish hand
and then a pale leg. She was tall and slender with shoulder-
length blond hair. The TVs miniaturized and multiplied her.
Through her dark reptilian make-up, there was some sense of
the young girl in the portraits at Pig's and, more amazingly, of
the woman I had seen bathe in the fountain. Madison moved
her torso smoothly, twisting her arms at right angles, like a

soldier. Her belly vibrated as she spread her legs before the crowd. The black light made her skin seem rich and flawless and emblazoned her white lipstick and the wide eyes painted surrealistically over the material of her top. She was a psychedelic dream.

I pressed to the front of the crowd. Dancing in a slow introspective way I thought might attract her. This is the first thing, I thought, doing whatever is necessary to attract someone. Sweat soaked the material over her breasts and they slowly became visible, each nipple pierced with a slender gold ring. Her pants became translucent and I could see the dark ringlets of her pussy. My palms were wet and I found myself staring at her stomach. I wasn't sure if I wanted her or wanted to be her. The music broke down and she swung her hair. She never looked at me, just danced harder until the music ended with a sound like a bomb exploding. She fell to her knees and threw her arms back, lifting her torso in offering to some huge tongue. The light extinguished on a rising cloud of smoke and she disappeared. The industrial dance music began again and the crowd loosened, returned to conversations. I felt light-headed, disoriented, because I felt attraction for Madison instead of the pity I had anticipated.

She appeared at the bar about ten minutes later with a fresh layer of white lipstick and without the dark eye make-up. Her body was fragrant and delicately flushed. She wore a sleeveless silver mini-dress and white go-go boots that laced up the front. I felt giddy to be so close. I watched her neck pulse as she drank from the slender cocktail glass. She caught me staring and smiled, placed her drink firmly on the bar.

For a moment I forgot why I came and cast my eyes stupidly down. Her hands were puffy like Pig's.

"I know your mother," I said. She flinched and I realized I should have started slowly, told her I liked the performance, asked her name.

She smiled, but all her emotive energy cut off, black screens went down in her eyes and she turned back to the bar. It took me a second to realize she wasn't going to speak to me. Bar noises grew louder; copulating voices, driving disco, the sound of breaking glass. I pressed my side against her, felt my nipple harden but still she didn't turn, so I bent and whispered, "She sent me."

"Are you her new girlfriend?" Madison looked over her shoulder as if something about me physically might explain why I had come.

"I do some shopping for her, a few chores around the house."

"I bet," Madison said, smiling at the bartender.

"She's your mother. She wants to see you." I didn't like my earnest whiney tone of voice.

"That's really what she told you?"

I nodded.

"My mother is dead, both my parents died in a plane crash." She spoke so blankly it was impossible to tell if it were true.

My eyes welled, not because I felt sorry for Madison, or that she was being cruel by playing with me, but because it seemed the facts I trusted were lies. I felt awkward, stupid, tears came and I saw Madison realize this and reach for her silver bag.

"Go to my apartment," she said quickly. "Here's the key. You can tell me what's wrong with Pig later." She got a pen and wrote her address on a bar napkin.

HER APARTMENT WAS ON THE THIRD FLOOR OF A MASON STREET building. Her door grimy, patched with a square of raw wood. I knocked. No answer, just the faint rush of cars from the front window. The door next to Madison's opened and a fat woman in sweatpants came out, her hair pulled back tightly. She smelled of yogurt, and her face might have been pretty if it hadn't been so fat.

"She's hardly ever here," the lady said. "If you want to come in I'll write down where she works."

Over her shoulder I saw the inside of her apartment, posters of wrestlers and football players, mostly black. "I've already been there," I said. "I'm a friend spending the night."

She lumbered closer to me. "It's a sleazy place, isn't it?" She seemed excited. "Madison's a lap dancer isn't she? Not that I care, I'm moving soon. I don't want any of that AIDS shit."

When I tried to answer, the woman frowned, she had already decided what to say next. I was uncomfortable and stared at the crossroads where the woman's big belly and crotch met to make a T. This was how she got her thrills, I thought;

trying to shock people gave her intimacy with them. She looked at me sternly, deciding I needed to be converted, that I was a physical and careless person. The way she hesitated, I knew, too, that she was lonely, that she hoped we would talk forever. Sweat broke out on her upper lip, beaded on her forehead. I felt an instinctual disgust for the woman, and that repulsion must have passed over my face because she tipped her chin in like a child who is shy, then said, "Good-bye," stepped back into the forest of poster men and slammed the door.

I went into Madison's apartment. The overhead switch, the lamp by the bed and the bulb in the refrigerator were all burnt out, so I pulled the curtain back and let the street light illuminate the place. To say the apartment was shabby would be unfair. The falling plaster looked more like an abstract painting than simple decay, and the wood floors were worn smooth. The bed was covered with a rough wool army blanket, and above it was a knifish cubist painting. A blowfish suspended from the ceiling spun slowly on its line, first one way and then the other. The only furniture was a nightstand near the bed and a chest by the window.

I sat on the bed listening to street noise and the building's creaking pipes. Would Madison come and did Pig tell me the truth? I tried to think of them as mother and daughter, but the more I pushed them into that scenario the less likely it seemed a family had ever held them. But it's hard to think of myself in a family. And I, like everyone else I know, considered myself, even as a child, different, aloof, out of sync with the rest.

The fat woman ran her vacuum and I was reminded

intensely of the abortion I had had in college. The suck of the vacuum, the rich smell of blood, and how afterward I stayed in my room with the blinds closed and the lights off for several days. I had the sensation of being completely empty, like standing in your old room the minute after the last box has been carried out. I remember going outside in my nightgown to a bench in the sunlight. Nothing that came before that moment seemed real. As if I woke, not just from three days, but from a whole lifetime of sleep.

Patterns of barbed-wire light fell over the walls. I lay there listening to clicking high heels and men yelling to each other. I was sleepy and thoughts began to fragment. I remembered my mother in a special pale-green nightgown that she would wear when my father returned from business trips. In my mind's eye that nightgown grew and grew until it filled the corners of the universe and I slept.

When I awoke it was dark. The curtains had fallen and it took me a minute to sense the parameters of the room and remember where I was. Just as I did, the bed shifted, someone was beside me. I stiffened. At first, I thought instinctively that it was Bell, then more logically that it was Madison, but I knew by a certain musky scent that it was a strange man.

My back was to him, but I was close enough to feel his warm breath on my neck. I tried to calm myself, thinking he simply thought I was Madison and once he figured I wasn't, he would apologize and leave. There was an odd familiarity here, because I had used this fantasy a hundred times—being with a stranger in a strange room, never seeing his face as he took me from behind. I had a liquid sensation of ice melting into a shot of whiskey. The man slipped a hand between my legs and before I could think he began to undulate his fingers, sliding his other hand under my shirt. I pulled away a little and made a negative mumble, but he yanked me closer. His fingers were calloused and I could feel them slide under my bra, cradling the curve of my breast. With his forefinger, he rubbed my nipple until it hardened. He unzipped my pants, letting the heat of his finger-tips flow over my lower stomach. I was very wet, the moisture running into my ass.

All in a rush, he loosened his pants and his hard cock flapped against my spine. He rubbed it in the crack of my rear. Spreading his fingers over each breast, he pulled back, forcing me to arch, so he could lick my neck and shoulders. He moved his hands down to my hips, pulled my pelvis up and easily slipped inside. For a moment he was still and I listened to the footfalls on the stairs; it was long enough for me to rise to logic, think—*what is happening*, think, *kneel down*.

He began moving in spirals. A car alarm whined and another man coughed through the wall. I tried to pull off but he grabbed my hips back hard. I tried again, feeling the tip of his cock just barely leaning on the outer lip of my cunt before he pulled me back, gasped. I could feel his cock stretch and the arch of semen, felt dizzy and frightened, stood, pulled my jeans on and ran to the door. The stranger made soft disoriented sounds. The bed creaked. He leaned up and said, "Stay." I looked back a second, the light falling on his bare legs made them look scrawny and strange sprawled on the rough blanket.

THE NARROW GRID OF MY LIFE WAS CHANGING VIOLENTLY LIKE flood waters expanding the banks of a river. I was suspicious that I had let the stranger fuck me because I was intentionally trying to devastate myself, encourage confusion and misery, so that I would have no impulse to pose or lie. I felt I knew what was best for me, but that somehow, because of a certain well-practiced falseness, a sort of stupid conventional programming, I couldn't do it. But was I right to undermine my life in an effort to right it?

It didn't matter, because it hadn't worked. The first thing I decided was to lie to Bell. Not so much because I always thought I would, but because to keep the lie secret would give me strength. I used to lie a lot until I met Bell, who lied better and with more regularity. When you lie you take on the role of either self-promoter or coward. I was the latter, but to have a potentially hurtful secret would give me power. Lying is like violence in its momentary thrill.

Why lie? Wouldn't it be a relief to have him stomp off? But I didn't even know the stranger. He had about as much significance as a rat and it would be a bigger lie than not telling to pretend he had meaning. Also, I remembered Bell's audition, his threat to the couch, that he would torture me with his own infidelities.

The lobby of our building was painfully bright and the stairwell smelled of strange meat. I turned the key silently and immediately heard Bell's even breath. Though I knew he was asleep I still felt awkward stripping, like he was subconsciously checking for hickeys or wet hair between my legs. I got under the covers. *No man could save you from yourself.* I had a rush of remorse about what I had done. Maybe I had overblown our problems? Bell loved me and it was a wrongheaded sexual retribution that had lured me to the stranger. I let the traffic lull me, watched several planes on their way across the Pacific and thought how much better things would be between us now.

But then he shifted, pulled me closer, reached his hand between my legs and whispered, "You're so wet." The thought of sex with Bell in such proximity to the stranger was terrifying and I moved his hand and said, "I don't feel like it." It was so rare I refused that he persisted, moved his hand back over my cunt, worked his hips and cock against my rear, said into my ear, "What I love about us is that we're like gods." He slipped a finger into my cunt. I was worked up, felt the skin at the base of my neck get numb and pushed into his hand. Bell pulled my pelvis back and slipped inside with a wet sound. He tightened his hands on my hips. His breath quickened, he kissed the nape of my neck, said I had a tight pussy, that he wanted to come all over it, that he was going to come on my face. The dark was mucusy and all I could focus on was the dog skull on the ledge and the red exit lights in the hallway windows of the Hotel Huntington. I thought of the stranger and how he smelled like charcoal, how his cock was thick.

"Do you like it like this?" I whispered, "This is just what I did for the stranger." I pressed my pelvis back hard, thought of both men taking me at once. As Bell came, he shook me into a liquifying sensation, like honey rising up into combs. We lay there, until his cock softened and slowly slipped out. My ears rang and to keep from getting nauseous I looked for stars in the midnight blue sky above the hotel lights.

Bell was sound asleep. I couldn't get comfortable and I don't know if I had slept or not when I saw a man in our room. I gasped. It was Bell's little friend from the Black Rose. The light from the street illuminated the reds and pinks in his open mouth, he caught my eye like a fish hook, holding his fingers to his mouth. "Sssh," he said, "you'll wake Bell. Come see me downstairs." He stood, put his coat over his arm and walked quickly toward the door.

As the door shut behind him, Bell opened one dreamy eye, then rolled to the other side of the futon. I didn't want to wake him, or for him to interfere. I stood, pulled on my jeans, forced my feet into high-tops and buttoned my jacket over my bare chest. I found the little man sitting on the steps of our building. He blew smoke in the direction of the used-book store across the street and looked up at me. "Well." He stood awkwardly. "You're angry I stayed?"

I had to remember not to displace my anger on the little man: it was Bell who was the fucker. Why had he wanted to have sex with the troll in the room? Did he get off on the fact a stranger was so near? Did the little man masturbate along with us, rubbing his dick, waiting until he heard our breath quicken so we could all come together?

"I feel too stale and stupid to talk right now," I said. He nodded miserably, knowing something grave had happened.

There was that cantaloupe-colored light on the buildings and the digital bank clock across the street beat out the time. I felt like I had dirt in my heart. Irrationally I wanted to confess to the little man. "It doesn't matter you were there while we fucked. An hour ago I fucked someone I don't even know." Even the idea of telling the truth made my face flush and I pressed my hand over my hair.

"Let's sit down," he said, "on those steps there." We sat on the lowest step of a Victorian. He took my hand into his lap. It was like holding the cool hand of a child. We were quiet. He spoke in a deep voice that sounded strange coming from his tiny body. "Let me tell you about yourself. You're a girl from the suburbs. A good girl, not that you haven't done bad things. You've lied to seem interesting, complex, and it's worked, especially combined with your intrinsic charm. You still think of that cheap ranch house, the bedroom with white furniture and the mall you went to on Saturdays, browsing through discount records, drinking Orange Julius and buying plastic earrings at K-mart. You want to be different, not just from your suburban neighbors, but from everyone. It's not really megalomania, you just need to feel special in order to believe you are loved."

I started to open my mouth, though I had no idea what I would say. But the troll held his hand up. "Just let me finish . . . Your parents are divorced. With a girl you can tell around her eyes, boys have other ways of showing." My mind went away from the troll's voice. I thought how odd it was my parents were divorced. How one day I had a set of grumpy parents in a home that held the family archives and the next my father had married a younger woman and enthusiastically joined her family. And my mother was so bitterly furious in her little divorcée condo it was hardly possible for her to interact civilly with me at all. The little man talked on.

"Your father cheated before he left your mother. This has made it hard for you to trust men. But you're also suspicious that your mother undermined your father's love by scrutiny and mockery. You have noticed this trend in yourself and it frightens you."

There was a feeling like I was breaking up, blood seeping out of arteries, exposed veins moving like snapped electric wires. "If you're so good at this," I said, "what about Bell?"

He was angry I wasn't more appreciative of his magical trollish predictions. Stupid troll. Whether he had guessed or not, I would always think he had heard everything from Bell. I had a sudden vision of Bell in bed, his warm soft skin under the blankets, his head filled with erotic blue dreams. I looked at the little man still talking and thought, *What he is saying has nothing to do with me.*

I stood abruptly. He stood too, screwed his face up. He was going to have a temper tantrum like trolls do. And he did stamp his little foot and say, "You'll never be happy unless you learn to forgive." His neck muscles constricting, his little fists tightly at his sides, as if without absolute control they would start punching. I thought, *like a wife,* and turned, heading quickly down the hill. He grabbed my arm, whispered that I was a fool to hate people who were obviously one thing or another and by not choosing to be something completely I would end badly. "Watch out," he said, when I finally pulled away. "You don't want to become a fag hag." The thought hit my chest like a solid punch. The ones I knew had dramatic hairstyles, wore expensive tailored clothing and elaborate make-up. They talked loud, telling self-deprecating stories, then laughed drunkenly whether intoxicated or not. They seemed foolish and desperate, willingly abused by their gay friends.

I didn't want to go back to the apartment, so I walked over a few blocks and into Nob Hill. The streets were filled with cars and people coming out of their apartment buildings, hurrying to work. I saw a clean and attractive couple holding hands. I got close enough to smell her fragrant hair and his aftershave. They spoke in an intimate code and I thought of asking them if they would take me home. I followed until they kissed at the corner of Columbus and Grant and went off for the day in separate directions.

Chapter

Four

PIG'S HOUSE WAS DARK AND DAMP, THE ONLY LIGHT FROM twenty portraits of Madison lining the hallway. Lit dramatically, each had its own small brass fixture. Up close there was an angelic idealization around the lips and the colors of her eyelids were garish oranges and blues, creepy, matched with the babyish roundness of Madison's face. In one wide childish eye there was even a lumpish figure that resembled Pig. I originally thought a professional had done them, but it was clear now that Pig had drawn them herself. I heard a moan, looked up the stairwell and saw Pig's chubby hand flailed out through the slats of the banister.

"I'm flipped like a beetle," Pig yelled. The red nails of her fingers jerked and I could see, mashed into the banister, a lock of her hair and muzzy scalp beneath. I was scared at first. The woodwork under her fingers was stained red and a steady drip made a dark puddle near where I stood on the carpet. Holding my hand up, I caught a drop on my palm, a fragrant red wine.

"For God's sake, Jesse, hurry!" Pig yelled out. I ran up the stairwell to where she lay. Her kimono was tugged awkwardly up on one side, stained with wine and urine. A greenish vein beat in her pale forehead and her lipstick had dried in the cracks around her mouth. She grabbed my arm and tried to pull herself up a little. I had decided to be firm with Pig, chastise her for lying, give no information until I got some semblance of truth. But seeing her softened me, her fat fingers curled around my forearm, her cheek against my shoulder, she purred a little, seemed as happy as a child to see me. Besides, I felt pulverized from last night. Resolution, I decided, relied on distance.

I heaved her up by the waist, she hinged in the middle like a sack of flour, her head as loose as a rag doll's. Pig strained to arch her back, to get a hand up on the banister, to steady herself, but her legs folded under her and she slumped back lumpishly to the floor. "I'll never get up," she said breathlessly, "and I've made such a mess of it." She sunk her head into her hands, splaying her hair, the gray roots making it seem as if Pig had aged overnight. I squatted down, put my arm around her, braced myself against the railing and pushed up. This way Pig was able to get first one chubby bare foot under her, then the other. She rose slowly with one long moan. At eye level Pig looked into my face, trying to see whether I had found Madison. "It's better that I fell," Pig said breathlessly. "Just before I went down I started thinking I controlled everything; if I chose peppermint tea instead of lemon a car would crash on the highway."

Standing, she seemed strong, but as we moved toward the bedroom Pig's head slumped against mine. Her painted toenails dragged on the carpet. In the doorway she lunged toward the bed like it was the last rock before the waterfall. I propped her head up with the paisley pillows and opened the curtains to keep her oriented. Light shimmered on the tall cherry bedpost, highlighting the empty gilded frame over the bed. Pig was never willing to tell me what had been in the frame or why she had taken it out.

"It was horrible," she said. "I fell, tried a few times to rise, but then gave up and just lay there in the dark . . . Every now and then I'd hear a dog bark or a plane fly overhead. It was like I was a freighter ship going down and my earlier girl-self was on deck waving a yellow scarf."

I got her to lean up so I could peel off her rancid robe. Pig's body gave off the yeasty smell of bread dough. It was strange to see her; now that I suspected she wasn't a mother, her swollen body seemed even more embarrassing. I went down the hall to the bathroom and wet a towel with warm water. No matter how vulnerable people are, how fragile the delusional structure of their lives, they go on living. People die from liver failure, heart attacks and gunshots but not from loneliness, vanity or confusion—it was this obvious insight that startled me and seemed suddenly amazing. The water had gotten so hot it steamed up the mirror and made my hands numb. I wrung the towel out at its cooler edges and carried it down the hall. Pig's eyes had teared with relief and I let her wipe her face first, before I took the heavy towel and gently rubbed the hollow of her armpit. The hair was long and matted like winter grass. "You know, I was thinking of you and Bell last night," Pig said, settling down. "I remembered a man I knew who had homosexual tendencies, but went straight. His name was Neal. He worked as a cook, breakfast shift, then spent the afternoon picking up men on the beach." Pig paused, savoring the picture of nude men entangled on the back dunes. "Suddenly he became religious, decided he needed a wife, one with a couple kids—boys, I think." Pig's face animated as the details became vivid in her memory: smells, textures, shades of color. I knew how a memory could spiral off like loose yarn.

"The strange part was that when Neal married, his former boyfriend moved in with Neal's mother. He did things for her like grow tomatoes and fix her screen door. Last I heard he was nursing her because she had cancer or leukemia or something like that."

Her thighs were stained with wine. I opened the towel to the warmer middle. Her dry skin absorbed the wetness gratefully. Pig asked me to bring the robe hanging by the closet. It was a silky thing with a pattern of dogwoods and pink butterflies. She sniffed, leaning up for me to put it over her shoulders.

"I remember too, another time, when I was with my mother's friend. My father was gone for good by then, so I'm sure it was her boyfriend, but people didn't talk like that back then. He took me to a lake to swim and I sprained my ankle, but I didn't tell him. For some reason I felt embarrassed about it. When we got back, he walked ahead, but I had to go slowly, holding onto the car. Why was I so ashamed?" Pig asked me. "Don't you think it's strange?"

"Maybe something else happened that you can't remember?"

"No," Pig said. "It had to do with hurting myself. I think if someone had hit me or if I'd fallen it might not have been that way."

I nodded. Self-inflicted pain never gets much sympathy. You keep it to yourself. She grabbed my hand into her own sweaty one. I felt her quick pulse beat against my palm.

"Do you think the opposite of death is love or sex?" Pig asked.

"My father would say it's religion."

"Oh," Pig said, not particularly interested. "I always think of that story when Jesus turned water into wine."

The towel had cooled and I walked down the hall and put it in the hamper and got Pig some water from the bathroom tap. She took the glass gratefully.

"I had a vision, Jesse, but I shouldn't tell you because you'll just think I'm crazy." She hesitated for a second, long enough for me to notice the dramatic way she tipped her head and how her delivery took a coquettish turn. "I saw Madison and all these men were rubbing themselves against her."

I frowned. The dream was made up, the details too self-conscious, the meaning obvious—she was trying to lead me into talking about Madison. I wondered if everything she had said before was a strategy to mellow me, make me congenial to the upcoming interrogation. My unease showed and Pig's forehead wrinkled.

"Why are you so negative? It doesn't do you any good," she said. "Did you find her or not?"

If I looked into her eyes I'd be able to tell if she was lying, but this seemed cruel, so I walked to the window, looking toward the men in orange vests working on the BART tracks.

"Come on," Pig said, annoyed. "I've got to know."

I turned toward her. "She said you're not her mother."

Pig looked startled. "I was her mother!" she said in a high voice.

"Was?" I asked, walking over so I could look down at her restless face, all her features on one level like she had melted.

Her eyes became wide and wet, she fiddled with her wedding ring and another ring with a big obsidian stone.

"Well, I didn't actually have her."

"She's adopted?" I asked.

"Sort of," she said. Her eyes were unfocused, she was trying to decide what to tell me.

"What about your husband?"

Pig waved her hand. "He was long gone by then." She shrugged. "I don't think he would have been jealous anyway."

"You mean you had me track down your girlfriend?" I felt angry that Pig had lied to me.

"She was more my daughter than my girlfriend." Pig was getting flustered, the emotional complexity of her relationship with Madison was indescribable even to herself.

"Tell me what happened?" I asked.

Her eyes welled. "It's different than what I told you." She shifted and the bed swayed. "I saw her hanging around the big squat down the block; Mexican boys with skateboards and a few skinny white girls. She was eating out of the garbage, getting high, sleeping with everyone. Her hair was dyed blond, a good inch of brown at the roots. I saw her with this real evil-looking guy. Once they were smoking pot on the porch and he yelled at me to mind my own business, said I was a busybody. I couldn't care less about their drug problem, it was Madison who fascinated me. One day I gave her a cling-wrapped sandwich out of my grocery bag, then a couple apples, a bunch of little Costa Rican bananas, once a whole ham. It got so she would look for me. Finally one Sunday she rang my bell and asked if I needed any housecleaning done. She had cigarette burns on the backs of her hands and a big patch of hair was gone, her skin was raw and pink as salmon."

Pig smiled, but then remembered herself and looked to see if the story had touched me. It was hard for me to believe anything Pig said now.

"Did she seem curious about me?"

"She doesn't want to see you," I said.

Squinting her eyes, Pig pulled her loose features into a suspicious point. "Does she want to see you?"

Pig waited for an answer. Maybe Madison did, though I had no evidence to prove it. And besides, I didn't feel like I owed an explanation. I was disillusioned with Pig because she had lied, because she had used me, and because she seemed so pitiful now. She was a liar and a coward, so afraid that she was trying to make a safety net of her false connection with Madison.

"I know you're going to see her," Pig said. "Madison has a way of getting into your head." Her eyes moved around the room, as if the curtains or her hairbrush could help her.

I walked to the door, feeling dismal, concentrating on the open space in the hall and the darker spot down the stairwell.

"Don't you say anything!" Pig yelled from her bed. "You don't know what happened!"

FROM DOWN THE BLOCK I SAW THE LITTLE MAN COME OUT OF our apartment building. He ducked his head, looking cautiously around, hardly inconspicuous with that red hair. I wanted to be invisible, to follow him to his own apartment, to hear his lover yell at him about doing the dishes and where he'd been all night. What did he say to Bell? Did they long for their precious childhoods and fuck on the floor? Did they laugh about last night, and complain about me . . . "Bell," he would say, "all women care about is possession."

Inside the stairwell, a stench of pizza and urine came from the garbage chute. The knob was oddly warm as if the little man had lingered outside the apartment with his hand there. I used my key, careful not to jangle the chain . . . if I could catch Bell in some meditative position I might be able to suss something. But he was his public self, shaving at the sink. The room smelled of lime soap and cigarettes. I watched him turn his head, look for rough spots of beard, specks of shaving cream. He reminded me of my father. Shaving was one of the things that convinced me my father was more important than my mother. It made me feel safe to watch my father shave, that small act somehow held back chaos and kept harm from me. Bell's smooth pink skin seemed excited by the blade and the dots of blood on Bell's neck reminded me of poisonous sumac berries.

Had the little man upset him? Did Bell tell him about his father, how lonely he was near the end—so desperate he took to playing taped phone calls over and over just to hear a friendly voice. I tried to see if Bell's hand was shaking, if his eyes had gone blank.

"What did he say to you?" I asked.

Bell caught my eye in the mirror, waved his hand musically. "That I'm to end badly in a one-room flat with a dangling bulb, playing 'Tracks of My Tears.'"

"That sounds like your idea."

"He's no different than anyone else, he just says what you want to hear."

"Why didn't you tell me he was here last night?" I tried to resurrect some empathy by thinking about what I did with the stranger, but it didn't work. I wanted to make Bell admit he had perverse reasons for letting the little man stay, that these reasons had to do with his interest in boys. Was Bell motivated by jealousy? He knew I'd been with the stranger, though he didn't know yet that he did.

He smiled sheepishly, leaned back against the sink. "Because I'm miserable." He said this so calmly, as if he had said, "I saw a cute little dog today," it frightened me.

"About what?" I asked, though I knew he didn't have one answer. His eyes went away from me and he sat at the table fiddling with a spoon left over from breakfast. Was he thinking of how Kevin would look in a tux? How he would feel near his bride? Bell lowered his head. It was Kevin.

"Sometimes I hear a ringing like a soft bell and it always takes me a minute to realize it's my own heart."

"I think you should move out," I said. His incessant adolescent melancholy made me sick.

"Because of him?" He looked up.

"Because you're faithless. All you can do is dream about old lovers."

He softened his features, looked at me like I misunderstood him. "Kevin and my past," he said carefully, as if speaking to a child, "are no threat to you."

"You don't make me feel safe," I said. Bell had started to feel more like a brother than a boyfriend.

At this he stood, moved toward me, grabbed my shoulder. "I can hardly take care of myself," he said. When he saw my expression didn't change he stepped back and shook his head. "Let's face it, your time clock has gone off, it's ringing like a car alarm, all of a sudden you want a big house in the country and lots of children."

"You know it's not that. Tell me," I spoke slowly, because I was angry and didn't want to slur my words, "that I am the last thing between you and the total homosexual life you fear."

"I can't believe you're saying this!" He brushed by me and went into the bathroom, locked the door behind him.

I stood very still, heard Bell run water into the sink. I knew he was running cold water over his wrists, he was convinced this calmed him. I went into the kitchen and got a shopping bag from under the counter, noticed the metallic container of Ajax, the mousetrap still baited with an old piece of Brie and the flowerpot full of white granite that Bell had used to force narcissus bulbs last winter. The morning light seemed suddenly bright and the paper cracked loudly as I loaded underwear from the shoebox I kept at the top of my closet. I took T-shirts and a sweater. I went to the alcove, to the little marble-top table where I left my keys. I heard Bell fidgeting behind the bathroom door.

"I'm breaking up," he said, "and no one cares."

I thought, *Even love has its limits,* and I couldn't believe this hadn't occurred to him. Hadn't he learned anything from his parents? Lovers? Even friends? You had to act a prescribed way to be loved. I heard him shift his body weight and the water stop. Putting my lips to the cool paint of the door I whispered, "You can't have two lives, Bell. You'll ruin everything and we'll both be left with nothing."

I LIT SEVERAL PRAYER CANDLES IN GRACE CATHEDRAL. ONE FOR Bell, one for my mother, my father, his wife, her kids, one for

Madison, one for Pig, one for myself as a little girl. Then I lit a few for abstractions: courage, honesty, sanity and kindness. The flames rose from gold glass cups. I emptied my pockets of change, let the coins plunk into the tin box. I thought of all the other places candles burned, in Hindu temples, little Chinese dens, the formal gardens of Japan, satanic churches in the California hills. I thought of apartment fires where the dead are laid out on the sidewalk and of the blue gas crown on the oven at Bell's.

I knelt at a side chapel, the lushest one with a purple fairlane, rosette windows and a life-size crucifix. There was incense and a big vase of roses and violets. The stone walls were draped with tapestries, biblical scenes: the raising of Lazarus, and Rachel by the well. The miserable Jesus looked like Bell, though there was something knowing around the eyes I attributed to my father. Maybe it was because he was a minister and, like dogs and their owners, they had begun to resemble one another.

My knees were mashed into the burgundy cushion. I looked up at the figures of saints. Some of the women's expressions, an ecstatic submission, reminded me of the expressions on posters outside X-rated theaters. I remembered the story of one saint, a virgin, who cut off her breasts rather then succumb to a rapist. I made myself think *God is dead,* but it seemed dangerous. Then I thought, *my pussy is the same color as the carpet.* This comforted me somehow. I relaxed a little, saw how the sepia light from the window shone on Jesus's face. I knew that it was comforting to have someone around who knew all the bad things about you, the horrible things in your past . . . like a lover or a close friend, and I knew this was the purpose and place of Jesus. I took down the cord and walked to the altar. I stared into Jesus's raised eyes, then pushed my hips into his pelvis so it rubbed on the carved girth of cloth. A tightness came. I kissed his forehead, his upturned eyes, his open mouth. My tongue wiggled between his parted lips, I pushed against him and the cross rocked. Inside my tongue scraped the rough unlaquered wood. I tasted blood and sprang back, saw, like the momentary confluence of stars, how everything was connected . . . my father fucking around, my embittered mother, Bell fucking boys, me fucking the stranger, my own phantom longing . . .

CARMEN'S WAS DARK. I HAD TO STAND BY THE DOOR, LETTING my eyes adjust to its shimmery walls. The bartender mixed drinks in two silver cups. There was no music, just the continuous white noise from several televisions. I ordered a shot with a beer back, then asked the bartender, an older woman with spiky hair, what she knew about Madison.

"She's a girl like anyone else." She shrugged while drying a highball glass. The place seemed less exotic than last time. I drank fast and scanned the black-light murals. The nearest one was of an alligator leering at a nude woman. I ordered another shot, watched a drunken couple make out at the end of the bar. The man squeezed his fingers between her legs, then smiled like an idiot. The woman's hair was dirty, strains separated in shiny red cords down her back. Each time they pulled apart, they drank quickly and seemed ridiculously shy.

For a while, staring at my paper bag of clothes, my freaked-out eyes in the mirror behind the bar, I convinced myself I would go back to Bell. He was the only man that ever made me feel in life instead of just a spectator, and if he did that by fear and pain, it was still better than when I looked numbly at some man on the couch thinking, I will leave you soon. I got another beer and thought of Bell and me in a big apartment on Nob Hill, how we would have dark paintings and beautiful wooden bowls. Bell would have a job producing movies and I'd be a photographer and we'd eat tabouli and make our own Christmas cards and name our baby India. Our bed would be thick with patterned blankets, quilts and cranberry satin pillows. But the dream place bled into a starker room, Bell asleep on the futon, me awake at the window—our life as raw and painful as a bloody bone.

I was still angry about Bell's reference to my biological clock. To think of it was ridiculous—an old-fashioned alarm, that seemed a cartoon of the real angst . . . a vague sense that it was time to change. It began with noticing babies on the street, their funky sweaters and adorable little shoes. I noticed pregnant women too, how they seemed so positively preoc- cupied. And after so many lovers, the purity of the mother-child relationship became so appealing: there was no doubt your baby loved you. There was embarrassment too, at still being a maiden, because there were women in the beginning of that stage, fresher, more energetic and better at it than me. This sometimes made me feel ridiculously jealous. The biological clock was a feeling that it was time to move from one phase to the next, more advanced one. It was a positive and mature thing really, though men made it sound like a nervous disease.

But what had I done to stabilize myself? I had begun a relationship with a bisexual man, and as far as economics I hadn't done much in the last year except take some photos, sew the occasional hat or vest. Instead, I hung out in the cafés on 16th Street, pretending to read *Flowers of Evil*. The Mission seemed like the last bohemia in America, moved in the sixties from North Beach to Haight-Ashbury, both of which were overrun now with tourists looking for Kerouac and Cassady in City Lights and the Grateful Dead and the Drug Store in the Haight. The Mission was dirty, you could still get a two-dollar burrito, sit in the Albion or the Uptown, watch leftist documentaries at the Roxie. Used-clothing stores were not vintage and there was a host of prophetic street people who drank coffee and wrote manifestos in the cafés. One, a thin man named Spoons, sat in the Piccaro Café, distributing to everyone xeroxes that demanded life-time driver's permits, converting all the storefronts to squats and allowing girls to marry as early as ten. He also insisted that every light bulb had a tiny camera inside and that it was a CIA plot that he never got any mail. The Piccaro with its headless-Barbie-doll art, people in oversized sweaters scribbling into notebooks, reading, playing chess. It seemed authentic, but I couldn't decide whether they were posing or if I was. This scene and every other seemed hopelessly self-conscious to me. I felt as suspicious about bohemians as I did about professionals in upscale restaurants or suburbanites who catatonically roamed the malls of Palo Alto. I had come here to be different with all the others, but it wasn't working. Maybe it had to do with sheer numbers. It was easy to convince myself in Virginia that I was an interesting person, but here I was no different than other women. I couldn't help thinking that thirty years earlier we'd be married, cooking, knitting, arranging furniture—raising a family. Don't misunderstand me, there are obsessed and brilliant women artists in San Francisco. It was just that coming here made me realize I wasn't one of them.

Where would I go now? My mother would buy me a ticket home. When I got there she'd load blankets on my bed and bring me juice. I could masturbate while listening to suburban husbands mowing their lawns. I could go back to Pig. I smiled at the thought of them as my only alternatives. I thought of things I could do in San Francisco; cafés, museums, the park. Then I thought about where I would go if I could drive. I thought about all the towns I had lived in and what I did in each of them. But nothing would satisfy me, there was nothing on this earth that could settle me now.

Madison came down the side steps. There was a silver tear pasted near one black eyelined eye and she wore hiphuggers and a studded belt as wide as a fist. She didn't see me, which I found hard to believe as I was conspicuous as a cow in this robotic place. I yelled her name as the door sucked shut behind her, then jumped up and followed her out onto the wet street. She bent over, unlocking her car door.

"Why didn't you come?" I said to her back. She turned, slacked back against the car sardonically. Her eyes frightened me a little. And I noticed, too, how her biceps were full and rounded. She had the twilling vibrancy of people in good shape.

"Did Pig tell you she wasn't my mother?"

I nodded, realized how stupid I must seem to her and felt embarrassed by my dirty jeans and black high-tops.

"I came to ask you something." I took a step closer. She was like a cobra and I felt if I could get close enough to stare into those horrible eyes I could charm her.

"Why don't you just leave me alone?" Madison said. I was startled at the thin exhausted quality of her voice.

"I need some advice," I said.

She squinted at me. "Why do you think I could help you?" She asked like it was an impossible and crazy thing.

"I don't have any place to stay." It wasn't what I expected to say, but I realized now it was the reason I had come down to Carmen's.

She smiled. At first it reassured me, but then her lips spread in an expression I imagined a man might use on a young girl.

"You just don't get it, do you?" she said. But she seemed pleased. "You want to stay awhile, with me?"

I nodded. She got in and motioned for me to get in on the other side. It was a strange car with large rhinestones pasted all over the dashboard and a voodoo doll hanging from the rearview mirror. She turned the key in the ignition, her jewels caught light like broken glass and the radio played the same white noise as in Carmen's. Madison seemed to like it, she pushed the car lighter in, rifled through her purse, found her cigarettes, knocked two out, offering one to me. I bent toward her hand as she lit mine first, then hers off the fading coils of the car lighter. "You'll see," she said, absently plugging the light back in, "there are a million ways to kill off the soft parts of yourself."

Chapter

Five

I WENT HOME LATE IN THE MORNING BECAUSE I KNEW BELL WAS at work. I had slept badly at Madison's. A dream of cockroaches crawling into my mouth haunted me and I was worried the stranger would be suddenly beside me, his thick cock nudging my ass. At dawn the couple upstairs started fucking. The woman made a sudden bark of discomfort, but the man coached her into pleasure saying, "Like this. Just like this."

The apartment wasn't much different than when I'd left yesterday. There were still dirty glasses in the sink and a warm smell of eggs mixed with the clove cigarettes Bell lately favored. The ashtray was filled with butts smoked super low the way poor men do. But the place was already bizarre, the Bible opened to the Easter story and a mazelike drawing tacked up over the bed. The sheets on the futon were tangled. I hoped it meant Bell had slept badly, but to me they implied passion as well. With Bell there was always this OTHER. We never spoke of it, but I knew he was more excited with me after he saw someone dancing at a club or when he saw a man or a woman on the street he admired. And when he encouraged me to wear lingerie or get my hair cut short like a boy's it really wasn't so I would look sexy, but so I would resemble this other, an erotic abstraction in his head.

I broke the seal of the pint I had bought across the street and drank. There was something sustaining about the cold glass lip and the hot taste of bourbon. It was harder to break down the apartment than it had been to leave, there was something torturous about initiating the ritual of MINE and YOURS. I got the packing tape from the odds-and-ends drawer in the kitchen and put together the boxes. Loading quickly, I packed my shoes, several ratty sweaters and a blanket. I got the tiny wooden treasure chest my grandfather had made me and the paper-weight with the white rose inside. I took my lithograph of the angel, my old felt hat and the tea strainer from the kitchen. Sorting through the silverware drawer for my favorite spoon I felt my heart beating hysterically. I got in the closet, sat against the far wall looking out into the room. Remembered how Bell had once lured me out of here, from what he called my poodle bed, by putting a cream puff on a plate on the floor. And how my parents had divided their belongings: my father left first, then asked my mother formally in letters to send a certain photo, his suit with the cuffed pants, his old jazz records. Sitting in Bell's aroma, rubbing his materials against my cheek, I decided that all this was my fault because I was the worst kind of person; a pretty girl with high expectations who wanted more, but couldn't define more and prayed it wasn't just a matter of marrying money. I heard the incessant traffic on Bush Street, thought of heroines in novels. They were always optimistic and naive whether they were old women or whores. They were always beautiful, as if only the lovely had courage enough to go out into the world. They were smart in a dumb way, that inarticulate intelligence men seemed to like. They did crazy things because of love and in the end always realized something stupid that was obvious all along.

I skimmed every inch of the twisted sheets for sperm stains, worried that Bell had already taken a lover. Was it true that a man who really loved you would wait before he took new lovers? Or would the more desperate man seek a new lover immediately? Lately, I didn't trust the typical maxims of love, I know I sometimes loved men I cheated on more than ones I'd been true to. And besides, what did it mean that I didn't want him sleeping with anyone. It seemed territorial, had more to do with my will than any feeling for him. But that's the way it was with Bell from the beginning. It was his old girlfriend that started my obsession. I decided I wanted him once I'd heard about her: that she was five years older, had bleached blond hair, could speak French, that her father beat her and probably, most importantly, that she still wanted Bell. It was around these ridiculous facts my obsession with him flowered. But that wasn't really true, because when I thought of his lovely genitals, his narrow face, how he smiled with pleasure when I talked, how his body was warm, how it seemed to love me, I knew that I loved Bell, not only the mystery that surrounded him.

I spotted Kevin's wedding invitation lying under the table and crawled out of the closet. The envelope was worn fuzzy along the opening. I found a picture of Bell I liked and stuck both into my cardboard box. The two boxes and a green trash bag were all I had. It pleased me, I was like a monk or a disciple, I didn't need but a few bits of clothing. But staring at the sheen of the plastic I felt miserable. I was twenty-nine, and if I accumulated things at the same rate until I was ninety I would only have six boxes and three trash bags. But what did it matter? I wanted to stop thinking that accumulating things— people, houses, cars—could comfort or save me. But the thought of having nothing scared me, it was too much like being dead.

I dragged the bag to the lobby, then carried down the boxes, thought of sliding the key under the door, but decided to keep it. I might feel like spying on Bell or things could get desperate and I might need to sell my books or my radio. It was damp on the front steps. I sat there in a stupor trying to decide if I should flag a yellow cab or go back up and call the gypsy car service.

A cab came around the corner and I stood, motioned for it to stop. The driver pulled over, he was a congenial Arab who helped me load my things into the trunk. In the shadow of the cab I could see the I.D. card with his photo and his name—

Amud. His smile was well practiced as he asked about the framed photo I carried on my lap.

"It's my mother," I said. "She was Miss America and later became a doctor." The cabbie looked at me through the rearview mirror, first with lifted eyebrows in an expression of sudden interest. But when he saw how my mouth was loose from drinking and the crazy glaze covering my eyes he hunched his shoulders and drove faster. I often lied about my mother, as if saying what she might have been could somehow help her. Bolstering my mother was like pretending your boyfriend loved you. I leaned my head against the window frame, letting the cool air dry the perspiration on my face. This upset the cabbie.

"Your father, he helps you?" The cabbie turned toward me very slowly, trying to see if he could sense the refinement that was usually under the hippie clothes of young San Francisco women.

"I'm on my own," I said. This seemed to bother him. He pressed the gas, shook his head.

"A girl should not be like you are." I wanted to answer but couldn't think of anything to say, and the cabbie didn't look at me again. He turned on the radio to a channel with scratchy Arabian music and drove anxiously, revving the engine and edging forward at the lights. At Madison's he helped me unload my stuff, shaking the trash bag to see if I was crazy enough to move garbage. He took my money and drove off toward Market Street.

Upstairs I could tell Madison had been there. She had

left a portable TV and some sprayed carnations in a milky vase. The flowers were ugly and when I turned on the TV there was only aggressive static like the TV sets at Carmen's. These things frightened me and made me wonder if Madison had really meant to make me feel welcome.

I placed my grandfather's chest on the TV, tacked my Kandinsky postcards over the nightstand, draped a scarf over the headboard and leaned my mother's photo against the wall. It's amazing how a well-placed scarf and a photograph can transform a cement-block hotel room or a studio like this from any place into some place familiar. I dumped out the trash bag, folded my clothes into the drawers. The room still seemed creepy with the fake wood dresser and the metal institutional bed. Even the cubist poster was angular and soulless like a machine. There were distant sounds of activity in the building. It conjured up the last person who lived here, a little man with bad teeth who ate sardines and read cheap pornography. He had a heart attack in the tub jacking off. "There is nothing so lovely," he thought, "as a very young girl."

I crushed the boxes with my foot and stored them in the closet, certain this was only transitional. Madison's closet was spectacular, like a rack of costumes in an actor's dressing room. There were beads and belts—one nail alone for crosses and rosaries. There were no current-style clothes, which made me wonder if Madison might be older than I thought or maybe ageless like a vampire. I fingered the rich wine-colored velvet, smooth white satin, her colored vinyl, decided to try some on. First a sleeveless mini-dress. When I stepped into my reflection

I thought I was my mother. This was the style I remembered her in, or maybe it was this scenario, because I used to go through her clothes, smell her perfumed bras and slips—lie on her bed thinking of her body with my father's. But I looked more like Madison than my mother and I thought how malleable women are, with clothes they can look like virgins or whores or housewives. Their earrings give information, hemlines speak, eye shadows imply. I remember how Bell sometimes ridiculed my big sweaters and jeans, said I looked like a student. He'd point out women he thought were fashionable, usually ones in well-tailored black clothes. Sometimes I wanted new clothes, but when I stepped into little gray dressing rooms with the hooks on one side and mirrors on the other, the store's fluorescent light blaring underneath the door, I felt vulnerable and stupid and it was impossible to decide on anything.

There was a scrap of newsprint with Madison's handwriting scrawled all over in the dress pocket. I wanted to read it, but heard the door rattle and a key in the dead bolt. Madison came in carrying a tube of toothpaste and a package of toilet paper. She was startled to see me in her dress but didn't say anything. Instead she went into the bathroom and ran water to brush her teeth. I quickly pulled the dress off, turned to find my clothes on the bed.

"Nice butt," she said. "You could make a lot of money with a butt like that." Madison laughed, flopped down on the bed, watched me pull up my jeans. "What's your story?" Madison asked.

"I'm just a girl like any other."

Madison smiled. I could see I pleased her and I wanted deeply to do so again.

"Have you ever had an abortion?"

"Yeah," I said, "once in college." It seemed a strange thing for her to ask me. So quickly she reduced people to two things, their most violent experiences and their sexual desires.

"Sobering, ain't it?" she said, scanning the things I put up around the room. She fingered the blue silk scarf.

"Where are you from?" I asked.

She looked at me to show how easily I slipped into formalities. "Carson City. Aren't you going to ask me what my daddy does?" She smiled. "My mother said he was a cowboy but she's a liar. Another time she pointed to the guitarist on a video and said that was my father. My second stepfather moved us around a lot, crazy places like Spokane and some place in Mexico. He sold things: tanning beds, fire alarms. I've lost track of them now and we will never find each other."

"That's too bad," I said, though I knew it wasn't what she wanted me to say.

"I wish I were a lizard hatched in the desert sun."

I sat down on the bed by her feet. "I'll only be here until I get a job."

"You're going to work for me. Come over to the bar around one o'clock tonight." Standing abruptly, she moved toward the door. "Did they wake you?" she asked, pointing upstairs.

"It sounded like he was hurting her."

Madison shook her head. "She just pretends because he likes to think he's hurting her."

After she left I listened for her footsteps on the stairs, then on the sidewalk until they mixed with others and became untraceable. I looked at the clock. There was an intolerable pain connected with time now. I thought of drinking. I thought of masturbating, of watching a man fuck me in the ass, screwing me like a dog. These fantasies scared me now. I couldn't always control the men. They did horrible things, their faces contorting in evil pleasure.

The phone rang and when I answered I could tell by the heavy breathing it was Pig. "Madison," she said, "Madison, is that you? Don't torture me, it took a lot to call you," she said loudly. "I want to see you. I sent a girl, but I couldn't tell her what I really wanted to say . . . I know you're there . . . could you come out here, honey? Could you?" The helpless sound of her voice made me feel cruel and I whispered, "You're a fat old fool." When I said it I heard a sharp intake of breath and a sound like she had fallen against a table and the phone rattled onto the floor.

I felt bad, but no way could I call back to apologize. So I called my own mother. She answered on the first ring and told me excitedly that my father's cousin had died. "I always liked him so much," she said, "so what if he left his wife for a year or two and ran off with his secretary, when that was over he came right back to her. They got married again and everything. There is something primal about first love."

She allowed men their wanderings if they were rich or if they eventually smartened up. She wasn't exactly a situational moralist, more a financial one. I told her we had moved. She took the number and I said I had to go. She pretended I hadn't spoken, said, "The crazy thing is since I found out he died, I've been buying things. Just yesterday I bought a stereo and today these little Persian rugs for my car—I feel free." She giggled girlishly. I told her again I had to go.

"Why do you always call me when you have so little time to talk?"

"Sometimes it makes me sad to talk to you."

"Because you're afraid you'll turn out like me?"

That wasn't it exactly, more that her equation seemed tragic in such a trivial way . . . drunken father, no-good husband, that once she was beautiful and now she was fat, that she probably hadn't had sex in ten years, that her life had shrunk to a dollar sign. It was the only currency she felt comfortable dealing in, it was the only thing she trusted. "No," I said. "You just remind me I'm going to die."

"And get petty in the meantime?"

"Good-bye, Mom," I said. As I hung up I heard her say, "You're no different than anyone else, Jesse."

I lay on the bed, watching the light fall. I could see a sign across the street that said GirlsGirlsGirls. Above it a window with green drapes. The moon was rising over the brick skyline, outlining the highway ramps by the water.

I remembered Madison's note, heaved up out of bed and

got it from the pocket of the mini-dress. I could still read in the half-light.

> *I was pregnant, on X, couldn't really focus on anything. Boys kissing in the corner. I couldn't get into the bathroom to take a piss and stood waiting in line, watching a tall thin boy spin around so that his skirt flew up showing his net panties. When the door finally did open two girls and a boy in a red sequined sweater walked out laughing. There was a strobe that made me happy, until I saw in its pulse my boyfriend with a girl on his lap. I turned my head—that is his way—I said eight times fast and then faster until it went with the music and did not seem so bad.*

I put the paper into my little wooden chest, latched it, set the alarm for midnight and turned out the light.

THE BARTENDER TOLD ME TO GO UPSTAIRS. IT WAS A RELIEF TO get away from the leering men at the bar. The stairs were steep, covered in bruise-blue linoleum. At the top was a white door with a black sign that said PRIVATE. I put my hand on the doorknob and there was a sudden buzz. I pushed it open. The hallway was dark and because I didn't know the geography of the place I stood still for a moment letting my eyes adjust. The air was warm and damp and I could hear the sound of bubbling water. I walked ahead. There were giant fish tanks set into the wall on either side, dreamy angel fish, transparent guppies and pencil-thin silver ones. The tanks alternated with doors and windows. Moving toward the spiral staircase, I thought the woman in the first window was a mannequin, but then she looked up. A well-practiced look, a touch of naïveté, a question, and the perfect amount of distance, the kind of distance that elicits desire. She wore a white corset, the same shade as the shag carpet. There were other women, one wore a blond floor-length wig. She spread her legs, showed me her rouged cunt.

The blue lights made it seem like the whole place was underwater. I climbed the metal stairs. Madison's room was huge with the same thick white carpet, round white couches and a bed with a fuzzy white bedspread. Madison was near a white table, sitting in a white leather bucket seat. She wore a baby doll nightgown and patent leather go-go boots and said without turning, "Could you help me?" She was carefully heating the bottom of a silver spoon with a lighter. She slapped her forearm, made a fist, told me she hadn't medicated herself yet this morning, asked if I would hold her bicep until she found a vein.

"Couldn't you use something else?" I asked.

"I want you to do it," she said fiercely, "NOW." She slapped her other hand against the table and I quickly clamped my fingers thumb to thumb around her upper arm.

"Tighter," she said, "these veins aren't for shit anymore." Her arm marbled, then turned pink, the veins puffed up and she finally found one she liked, in the delicate underside of her forearm. She loaded the syringe. I hated how the needle slipped in, as if her flesh were butter. There was a bloody backwash that tinted the heroin rose.

"Let go," she said, pulling the syringe out. She pressed a tissue over the vein, folded her arm up, then slid back into the chair. When Madison saw how startled I looked she laughed.

"You're not one of those people who consider seeing your parents argue intense?"

"I think seeing a seagull with a broken wing on the side of the road can be just as horrible as—"

"As what?" Madison asked. "Getting raped?"

"No," I said, "of course not. I just don't think there is a real hierarchy of pain."

Madison nodded. "Fair enough. So what's your opinion of blow jobs?" Her smile was not a smile at all.

"Do you have some kind of philosophy about them?"

Madison rolled her head dreamily toward me. I could tell the drug was taking effect. "Well, many powerful things seem based on them: rockets, skyscrapers, guns. But, in a way, they're all pitiful. When I have one in my mouth I think of it like a dumb worm. It doesn't know the difference between a cunt, a hand or a mouth. And while the men think I'm either servile or kind, depending on their feelings for me, I know that it's a service. When I give head, I'm like a mechanic. The cock is a car. The car's owner, just like the owner of the cock, knows nothing about me or how I really feel about him."

"It's all so esoteric."

"Esoteric?" she repeated angrily. "Tell me how you lost your virginity."

"No," I said. "Let's talk about my job."

"Tell me what happened, it's part of the interview," she said. "And sit down over here by me." She patted the chair near her.

I didn't want to tell the story and tried to change the subject by asking how tips were at the bar. She ignored me and said, "Please continue."

"O.K.," I said, "I'll tell you, but it won't prove anything."

Madison looked up slowly, her eyes were glassy now and she smiled.

"I rode the bus down to Georgia. It smelled horrible, because an old lady in the back had shit in her pants and I remember thinking how the trees and shrubs on the back roads seemed lushly malignant. He picked me up. We drove to a subdivision where he and other boys from the college had a duplex. We went up to his room, it was sparse, anemic with calculus textbooks in a metal bookshelf and a mattress on the floor. He undressed me and placed my hand on his little cock. Afterward, he went to the bathroom and I found a gold earring stuck between the wall and the bed."

"Let me tell you mine," Madison said, she sat up in her chair and reached for the light, turned it away so we sat more in the shadows. I thought of dark confessionals and how when I take a new lover I always dim the light. "Sometimes, just kissing I got so wet my underwear would be soaked. There was this guy. He told me he wanted us to have a baby. Sure I fell for it, I chose him over the other groping potheads. But after a while he kept bugging me to fuck, he would scream every time I said I wasn't ready. He started to talk in baby talk to me and he'd say I was the same as little girls we saw on the street. I got angry. And while he was away two friends of his came over and asked me if I'd have sex with them. I said I would and they took me to an apartment. I think it was one of their uncles'. It was empty with just a single lawn chair and a card table. I leaned against the wall and they fucked me one after another."

"And you never told your boyfriend?"

"No, we did it right after and I pretended to be a virgin."

"I feel sorry for you."

"Why? That's how I felt."

I was aware of being clichéd, sentimental and wanted to show her I could be as tough and raw as herself.

"What's the worst thing you ever saw?"

"My father with a boner." She laughed hard, then her face pulled up suddenly, as if she had thought of something horrible. "I'm not unwilling to die," she said, looking at me with sleepy eyes. "After a while the men who come around here seem as inconsequential as flies."

Chapter

Six

IT WAS A HARD NIGHT, MY ONE-WEEK ANNIVERSARY AT CAR-
men's. I got home around five in the morning. There was a
sliver of light creeping over the horizon. I closed the curtain
against it and lay waiting nervously for sleep. It wasn't sleep that
came, just levels of flattened consciousness, one moved into the
next as easily as lovers move toward one another in dreams.

I had expected the night to go as all the others: the slow
setup and stocking, the first customers, then the frantic rush
that lasted until closing, but tonight a couple of weird things
happened. First, Susan ran downstairs naked, her bare chest
splitting the crowd, swaying under the computerized lights. The
upstairs door banged open and Madison pounded down after
her. She pulled Susan by the wrist, twisting her arm so the girl's
head was nuzzled in the crook of Madison's neck. She got her
to the foot of the stairs before Susan stiffened her legs, grabbed

onto the railing and wouldn't let go. Madison touched her chin, whispered something in her ear and stroked her hair. Susan's eyes went soft and she let Madison lead her up the steep staircase. She looked at me just before the two of them disappeared behind the metal wall. It scared me because I couldn't tell if it was a warning or if she loathed me, felt I was Madison's accomplice. Then at closing, while I was wiping down the tables in back, this jerk came over, one who ordered slippery nipples all night. Each time he said the name he grinned like a sophomore in high school. He came back, offered me a five pinched between his thumb and forefinger. I didn't like how he folded the bill long ways, or how he held it slightly away, but I reached out anyway. Of course, he pulled the bill back and laughed. I noticed the deep red capillaries spidering through his cheek and how his beard was wet around his mouth. I shifted my eyes down to my rag and continued wiping wet ovals over the glass tabletop. There was something anemic about him, with his khaki overcoat. "Sorry, I didn't mean nothin'." He grinned sheepishly, revealing a sliver of chewing tobacco caught between his teeth. He held the bill out closer this time. Turn the other cheek, I thought and reached out for the money. But he pulled it back again. I scrubbed a sticky spot off the glass, picked up a swizzle stick and a napkin from the floor. The man just stood there holding out his money, his mouth clenched in a broad and scary smile.

The clock moved interminably toward morning. I opened the curtains a bit, the raw light reminded me of infected skin. Daylight was trying to trick me into thinking life was good. Instead, I lay in the dim light, listening to the early morning news on the transistor radio, trying to see what the people across the way were doing. I hoped Madison would come by today. I thought of telling her I loved her, not so much because I did, but because I was desperate for some elemental connection with her. Sometimes I imagined us in this bed, spooned together, her breasts pressed into my back, the soft hair of her pussy curling toward my rear. I knew I was lonely and that she made me feel inadequate, but I have always been attracted to people who make me feel inadequate. But I wanted to center my life on myself, not this continuous pattern of revolving around another. The first construction sounds of the day started down the block: the hum of the crane, a jackhammer. The workmen came to me, their tool belts flapping gently against their rears. I remembered how the stranger had held me from behind with an arm around my waist tight as a seat belt. I imagined Bell fucking Kevin, two young men connected in the missionary position. I tried to clear my head by staring at the water stain on the ceiling shaped like a daisy. I didn't like thinking of Bell connected to anyone but me. I thought about my former lovers. I remembered how a man was inside me and I was nowhere, and in an effort to arouse myself I would think FUCK ME, and just the visualization of those words, I wouldn't even have to say them, would send me over. That was the first time my sex life became two things—the mechanical sexual reality and the ongoing fantasy. The first fantasies were naive—a stranger licking my pussy, taking me from behind; each act I developed to the last detail, flat strokes of his tongue, his calloused fingertips on the goose-pimpled skin of my rear.

I pretended the morning traffic was the elemental purr of the ocean, thought of waves pulling away sand to expose coquinas. Their milky purple shells revealed for an instant to the sun, but then a mucusy muscle reached out and dug back under the sand. Finally, I was sinking into sleep. My mind's eye enamored with light moving over a huge crystal clamshell and over the face of the man that held it. Though the features were bland I knew it was the stranger. He told me in a whisper that the bowl held a thousand tears. He dipped his fingers, sprinkling me everywhere as if the water were holy. He told me that I was not alone. The clamshell rose then and floated transparently above his head.

THE NEXT NIGHT WORKING UNDER THE STROBES WAS DISORI-enting. I watched men lean against the walls, hips pressed out, eyes fixed on one woman after another. I chanted while mixing potions from the illuminated liquor bottles. In just one week I had become a judge of liars and learned about conquest—how a woman opens her body, lets her eyes go soft, how a man saunters toward her. I found that misery at its worse was quiet, how one moment swallows the next until it's the end of the world, closing time, when the little Mexican man mops up the floor and the whores come downstairs to drink sleepily at the bar. I saw too that the best-dressed men tip the worst, that men in toupees always demand fast service, and how a man who loves bourbon can be as grateful as a child if you pour him shots above the lip. If I made that trembling crucible which reminded me of the moment before you kiss someone, then they looked at me with the eyes of a lover.

I watched the clock, waiting for Madison. To me she was like a woman that stepped out of the sun. I wanted her brilliance, her ease, her power. Desire has two speeds: quick match flames, unpredictable as a wild bird stuck in a house, and slow-building long-term desires—a walnut kitchen table, hand-thrown mugs, the steam off the coffee wisping around the lip and a sleepy-looking man across from me with eyes the color of green grapes and long-fingered hands like a pianist's. But what did my worn-out dreams have to do with Madison? I knew people want most what they pretend to hate, that it takes courage to say what you really want. But Madison didn't want a normal life, she wanted to be perverse and powerful, to transform into a monster.

It wasn't until last call that Madison came downstairs and sat on the stool closest to the stairs. Her make-up was smudged, her fisted hands flattened against the steel bar trying to relax. Would I bring her a beer? she asked politely. I sulked, offended she had spoken to me like any other customer. I wanted to tell her I was desperate and lonely, but I knew at the beginning of relationships you couldn't show much need. If I did I'd be associated with the sad men at the bar. I suspected Madison was no different from anyone else. She had an animal sense that vulnerability is dangerous.

I brought her a beer, placed it neatly on a napkin. She asked me for another and when I brought it she asked to borrow my pen and began writing on the napkin. She held the pen loosely, looking up every phrase or two and letting her eyes sink back with thought. I watched her while pouring beers. It was getting to the point in the night when the drinkers get demanding. One accused me of watering down his drink and another said I overcharged. Madison leaned up on the edge of her chair. Her intensity made me curious. I went over, asked her if she needed anything else. She looked up.

"You saw Susan come down here yesterday?"

I nodded. "It was hard to miss her."

"She got spooked because a man she was fucking said his dick was a snake."

I shivered. "That's creepy."

"Hey," a man yelled, shaking his empty glass. Madison nodded for me to serve him. He snarled like a dog when he saw me make his iceless drink in a smaller glass. When I glanced up Madison was gone. But her napkin was there, as if she had left it intentionally. Stuffing it into my pocket, I called a lap dancer over, a heavy Mexican girl named Mercedes. She agreed to watch the bar while I went to the john.

The bathroom smelled like anxiety. I closed the lid on one of the two toilets and sat down, staring for a minute at my shoes against the checkerboard floor. I took out Madison's note. She had pressed so hard the ink had gone through several layers of the fine paper, each sheet with less ink so the second looked like Arabic and the last like a child's drawing of snow.

Susan said, *"He put a snake up inside me, I
can feel its scaly skin."*

"No," I said, *"that man was just tormenting
you—he likes to think his dick is a snake, but it's not
really a snake."*

*She clawed at her crotch so the skin tightened,
turned deep pink.*

"O.K.," I said. *"I'll get it out."*

"Where will you put it?" she asked me.

*I brought over a paper bag. She lay out on the
bed and spread her legs, I touched her cunt gently, then
pressed hard on her lower stomach and made a scream
like a TV evangelist, then pretended to throw the snake
into the bag, rattled the paper to convince her the snake
was inside, then ran into the bathroom and flushed the
toilet. When I came out she had her arms around her
knees.*

"It's over," I said. *"We killed it."*

"You don't understand," she said in her sad
voice. *"That old snake just comes and goes whenever it
feels like it."*

I know the girl is right because the snake is in me,
knotted around my intestines, hanging off my ribs, snuggled like
a lover around my black heart. "I love you," I said, addressing
the snake, Madison, Bell, Kevin, Pig, my mother, my past lives
and the new lover speeding toward me this very moment. I
wondered if it mattered whether you loved one person or an-

other. Weren't lovers interchangeable when you thought back about them? Maybe that was true in the future too. What I really loved was the note. I always loved odd things: the blue curaçao bottle, the wet asphalt, my own insipid fear.

SHOVING THE BEER GLASSES DOWN ON THE BRISTLE BRUSH, I practiced my calm voice, the one without the slightest hint of hysteria, the one that wanted nothing and would elicit Madison's desire. I counted out the money, stacking crumpled bills. Madison came down in street clothes, demure for her, bell-bottoms and a halter.

"Do you want to go somewhere for a nightcap," I asked.

She put her silver jacket on and told me she had to meet someone else. Before she finished talking I decided to follow her, afraid of what I'd do if I didn't get to speak with her tonight. As soon as she turned her back, I shoved the cash into the canvas bag and put it into the safe under the bar, asked the lap dancers to lock up.

Outside newspaper blew in hectic spirals and the sex-show signs clanged against their shorings. Her silver jacket ahead was like a fish that toys with the surface. She crossed McAllister, then Market. I thought she might be heading for Hotel Utah, but it was hard to tell, the way she zigzagged. Her route seemed random, but she turned her head up to il-luminated windows so often I thought she might be looking for a signal: a lamp, a particular picture on an apartment wall. Who was she meeting? A customer? Her drug dealer?

It was colder on this side of the city. The chilly air caught in abandoned warehouses and boarded up storefronts. I liked the shades of brick under the artificial light and the sound of cars speeding overhead on I-80. The cement columns were covered with graffiti and, at the base of some, homeless people slept in refrigerator boxes. I wasn't paying attention and had gotten dangerously close to Madison, who was waiting senselessly at the light. This didn't seem like her. I back-stepped, paused at the far end of the block for her to cross. Red to green, but she stayed put. Her jacket glittered, her profile too took a verdescent turn. Somehow, her strength made it possible for me to leave Bell. Bell's romantic interest in pleasure seemed docile now compared to Madison's insistence on transcendence through sexual stamina. I liked how she treated her sexuality—like a long-distance runner. Love wasn't important, endurance was all. What could it be like to live with those stretched and skewed standards? It reminded me of my own crazy standards, like the ten or twelve things my mother had taught me were pitiful: like slipcovers, bad perms, those change purses that open like tiny mouths. I wanted out from under these, because intrinsic in them was my mother's fear of poverty.

My eyes came back to Madison, leaning on the light pole like a teenager on a summer night. This stance which seemed somehow disingenuous reminded me of seeing Bell on stage. She stood like a person pretending to be alone, not one who felt truly alone. Maybe she was thinking of herself standing on the corner, maybe the image of herself gave her pleasure, or maybe she liked being observed, knew I or someone else was always looking. She yawned, rubbed her eyes sleepily, looked at her fingers, closed her eyes, moved her mouth quietly—then puckered her lips and blew. I imagined the eyelash propelled into the air, twisting and turning like a twig caught in a current.

She was so absorbed, so appealing. What does she wish for, love, money, a little bit of peace? My mother had taught me that a woman was most valuable before she had sex and that her virginity was mystically connected to her stability. But Madison believed the more sex a woman had, the more precious and powerful she became. I didn't move or call to her, but still I wanted Madison to sense I was there, to call me out. I wanted her to say my name, to promise me something. Watching her reminded me of Cybersex, a place on Leavenworth where closed-circuit TVs show a woman in bed asking the viewer what he wants her to do.

Madison looked up the block, to the right, then crossed the street. She was obviously waiting for someone. I thought of going around the block, pretending to meet her by chance. But it was somehow better if I watched her. It was this voyeuristic intimacy she loved. I walked back toward Market Street, saw the empty electric bus to the Castro coming toward me. I knew there was no way in the world I would sleep tonight.

THE BUS JUMPED ITS LINE, STOPPED, BIG BLUE SPARKS FELL PAST my window. The driver put on his gloves and went outside to connect the pole to the lattice of electrical wiring overhead. I could feel random electricity heating up my skin, upsetting my stomach, creating a tingly static in my head. I had to get off the bus, though the Indian man in the back warned me not to. He wore pukka beads and held a brown bag of Mad Dog in the low-slung pocket of his coat. He made me think how capitalism works best in the least-spiritual countries. In the Mexican deli on the corner I bought a quart of beer and some nougat the lady told me was homemade.

It felt good to be out. The air was fresh and occasionally I saw a fellow insomniac like myself. All this was mine: the dark houses, the liquid streets and the night clouds overhead hiding frozen stars. I walked past the Castro Theater, where a man plays the organ before the movie starts, and the Thai restaurant across the street where Bell and I always had salads with warm peanut sauce. Some things were familiar, but it still gave me the creeps to be down here. The artifice outside the buildings and the decor inside seemed overly ornate, even hysterical. In one gift-shop window homosexual merchandise was emphasized, a variety of cards with naked men and rubber penises with little feet.

I stopped: in a window I saw Bell at the bar, whispering intimately into another man's ear. A lizard slithered around inside my stomach. I could kill him, the way he leaned in and lay his arm loosely around the man's neck. I wondered if Bell preferred to sodomize or be sodomized . . . or was he a cocksucker? I suddenly felt dizzy and leaned up against the stucco wall. I wanted Bell to love me. A drag queen in a fur coat rushed by me and went into the bar next door. I followed her into the 500 Club. It was more crowded than the other after-hour clubs and didn't seem as seedy with its bright tiki lights. I sat there watching people pass. The jukebox nearby was filled with camp hits and Judy Garland songs, and there were framed photos of weight lifters hung against the black carpeted walls. I chose a still-warm stool by the door and ordered a bourbon. The young bartender, a Japanese man in tight white jeans and a half-buttoned tropical shirt, smirked when he set down my drink. There was a covey of leather monsters talking in the corner. I thought I recognized a few from parties at Pig's. Middle-aged men watched music videos, twisting their heads whenever the door opened. If you didn't count the drag queen I was the only woman here.

A fat man came in wearing acid-washed jeans and a baby-blue shirt open at the neck to show his gold zodiac medallion. He carried a shopping bag over his arm. A bald man he called Billy came to him and they both went to the back of the bar. The fat man slipped off his pants. The looseness of his skin and his black ankle socks reminded me of my grandfather. From the bag he took a black gown, as he stepped into it he told Billy that in Europe girls were wearing black dresses with fresh flowers in their hair.

"Zip it up," he said. "I want to see how it hangs."

"Oh, I know how it hangs," Billy said and the whole bar laughed.

Billy tried to zip it. He told the man to suck in. He tried to pull the sides together, but he couldn't get the zipper up.

"Oh well," the fat man finally said. A taffeta skirt didn't

fit either and he couldn't even get the satin wedding suit over his chest.

"That last one would have looked great on you," Billy said and walked back to his seat at the bar.

"I thought I was a perfect size sixteen and it's a shame because I can't return them," he said, his hands shaking as he folded the clothing carefully back into the bag.

"They didn't fit?" the bartender asked, trying to break the awkward silence.

"No," he said. "I'm getting too fat to be a girl." He grinned at Billy as he squeezed past a table to his place at the bar. He ordered a drink, then started talking about a man they both knew who had this boyfriend, Jeffrey, that couldn't be trusted.

The door opened again and a dwarf came inside. He put his foot on the bar rail and jumped up on a stool near me. Everyone knew him and said hello. His name was Hector and his little pants and white shirt made him look like a boy at his first communion. He ordered a seltzer, he said, because he'd been getting into trouble lately.

I ordered a double, slung it down hoping some man here would think I was reckless and come over. When I scanned the room there was a man who was watching, but he averted his eyes. Maybe I'd blown it or he'd decided I was a slut. He read a book, which was an odd thing to do in a bar at this hour. It made him seem like he wanted to delineate himself. Was he gay? He did remind me of Bell with his poised ambiguity. It was a well-cultivated masculinity tottering on the edge of femininity and it appealed to me so much. He was the sort of man Bell would fancy.

But maybe he only wanted to watch me. He turned a page of his book and sipped his drink, the ice hit his teeth awkwardly and he shot a side glance at me. I smiled. He smiled back, put his glass down on the table and walked over to order another drink. He got a dollar's worth of quarters to play songs on the jukebox. While he perused the selections I turned my chest slightly toward him, readied for the second I'd raise my eyes like the whores at Carmen's.

"It's all so camp," he said and shook his head.

I didn't answer. He asked me if I had a favorite.

" 'Sexual Healing,' " I said.

He liked that. I liked the way his pants hung loose around his hips and how he smelled like raspberries. He seemed very clean in his white T-shirt and new running shoes.

"Want to come over and sit with me?" he asked shyly. I nodded. He ordered me another drink and carried both of ours back to his table. He set them down, pulled out my chair and settled down in his own. I took a mouthful of bourbon. He closed his book—its plastic dustcover worried me—and leaned back in his chair, straightened his legs so the soles of his shoes brushed my bare ankle. He said his name was Jonathan. His expression was watchful and I wondered if I should have agreed to sit down.

"So why would you come to a place like this?" he asked.

I didn't like his tone and felt myself get angry, my voice

rise as I explained myself. "Because homosexual men fascinate me. That they only want each other, that they consider the same sex mysterious." I sipped my bourbon. The taste reminded me of desire. Jonathan sat up and leaned toward me, curved his open hand around his cheek and forehead, opened his eyes wider. "There's something wrong with me," I told him. "It's hard for me to be with regular men. I don't know why, maybe it's just that I like the demeanor of gays better. I don't like sports bars or rock clubs or the steakhead heterosexuals I see on the street. Besides . . . why does anyone go into the dragon's den?"

He smiled weakly, his mouth wet and slightly open. "We better go somewhere else," he said in a low voice. "I can tell that you're a complicated girl."

Chapter

Seven

IT WAS HALLOWEEN NIGHT AND THE STREET SOUNDED OF FIRE-crackers and shouting. I lay languid in the tub, watching vapor rise off the hot water around me. Steam swirled up through the candlelight. I bought the candles at a store across the street that always smelled of sandalwood and musk. They sold bone cruci-fixes, colored saint beads and little statues of St. Francis. The Mexican lady had scented oils for love or winning money, one called Fiery Wall of Protection and a smaller bottle of pink liquid called Guardian, which she said attracted angels to watch over babies. When I was sick last year Bell had bought a special remedy, a mason jar of green liquid. He'd opened the bottle, dipped his fingers and run them lightly over my feverish skin. There was a sudden smell of mint. The elixir was first cool, then warm, like a winter kiss.

I soaped a washcloth, slid it into the ridge of my rear,

pressing it just inside my anus, then rung it out and ran the bar of soap over it again until the material was thick with lather. Sliding the cloth into the folds of my pussy, soaping up the hair, I thought about douches and feminine sprays and the jokes high school boys used to make about women smelling like fish. What was it that made everyone so uncomfortable? Women worry that the scent reveals their sexuality and makes them vulnerable as dogs in heat. To men, the smell evoked the mysteries of the female body, which were cosmic but also threatening.

The cheap candles smelled of animal fat, dripping wax dark as ink on the porcelain tub. I let my hands, palms up, float to the top, the wrinkled tips breaking the surface. My hand had seemed separate when I jerked off the man from the gay bar last night. Each finger had a mind of its own and an eye in its tip. I watched the hand work on his cock, make an orifice out of fingers, squeeze down until he closed his eyes, imagining an ass as huge as the universe. Now the skin of my fingers was loose and gray as a cadaver. What could they be plotting? I wondered if the function of my body might be different from the function of my mind. I sensed the peace one found if they subverted either mind over body like a monk, or body over mind like a whore. You could hold both only if they were separated and severely so, like the right and left brain when the fissure is broken in surgery. I was trying by trusting my animal instincts over my intellectual ones.

Outside a man screamed something in Spanish. All good things are coming to an end, I thought, and though I knew it was true, I wasn't sure if I meant for me or for everyone.

Divorce had given me the horrific sensation that the two sides of myself were at odds. I am the worst kind of person, attractive, overeducated, raised with middle-class delusions of grandeur. But it's not just me; family life in America sucks, because if you're even a bit smart, the pressure from your family to jump classes is excruciating. There's this insane idea that materialism creates status. Even if you make some headway, it's an internal jump. You're always middle-class, talking on your cellular phone with your color TV muted. We should never have cast ourselves like gods, on TV or in movies—it ruined our memories, made us long and lust, in love now only with the image of ourselves. And perfected others: the nicest guys I see are characters on TV.

I've mesmerized myself watching the water droplets loosen from the faucet. They catch light before joining their multiple selves. There is a bit of motion at the edge of my vision, it's the snake. I've seen it moving in the drapes, shifting in the blankets.

THE RAIN STOPPED AND WARM MEXICAN AIR BLEW INTO THE streets. A little girl passed painted up like a whore, but it was too late for little girls. Ahead, on the other side of the street, a group of skinheads came toward me, angry about something. Hands deep in their pockets, they jumped on one another like monkeys trying to copulate. Some wore hooded sweatshirts and hockey masks over their shaved heads. A few carried baseball bats or cartons of eggs. I saw the swastikas on their jackets and the familiar White Brotherhood logo. I was wearing an outfit of

Madison's: red velvet bell-bottoms and a rhinestone-studded shirt and was worried they'd bother me. The tallest one, in a hockey mask, banged his bat against the brick wall. I turned, started to walk back the way I came when there was a sudden thud, then a burst like heavy rain. He'd shattered the window of the transvestite lingerie store. Tranced by the foam-filled bras and high heels as big as a strong man's work boot he reached in and took a garter studded with rhinestones. He looked like a monster holding a kitten. The skinheads were startled by the objects in the window which could so easily change them. A man came out from the next building in a ratty bathrobe, his eyes smeared with make-up.

"FAGGOT!" one screamed and they were suddenly on him. "Queer, butt blaster, fudge pirate!" They bashed his head against the hood of a parked car. The steely echo of the hood, absorbing the force of their fists on his body, made me shiver with nausea. It would have gone on forever but the police pulled up, lights flashing. One skinhead ran, then they all did.

"God damn," the man said, reeling. He touched his head where blood was matting in his hair. Another man came out from the apartment building in stretch pants and high heels. He helped the man to the doorway of the shop and held him while he sobbed.

San Francisco confounded me. First it seemed utopian, with the blue skies, pervasive Mediterranean light, palm trees, organic vegetable stores that sold strawberry juice, the children in funky handmade sweaters. But all that was an overlay—

misleading and cosmetic. Underneath was a history of deca-
dence: the opium dens in Chinatown, the thousand whores who
worked the gold rush, the voodoo and witchcraft shops. Even
the fast-moving fog was nightmarish. There were leather monsters fucking dogs and each other in the alleyways of SoMa and
the living dead haunting the Castro cafés. Sure, there were
hippies gentle and peace-loving, but there was also the Manson
family, the SLA and the Jim Jones Kool-Aid test. And California
is the outpost of rigid conservatism . . . the home of Nixon and
Reagan. Satanists are in the hills, chanting Latin, drinking urine,
forcing candles into the tops of rotten deer heads. And, of
course, there was Hollywood, the mimetic desire capital of the
world.

From way up the block Carmen's was explosive. Each
time the door opened, music hammered out and the crowd
spilled outside. Curtained windows upstairs had continuous
plays of light and shadow, which meant the rooms were occu-
pied. On the front door was a newsprint picture of a plane crash
and over it Madison had drawn the devil's eyes and a round
howling mouth. I paused for a moment with my fingers on the
handle listening to the pulse of music, knowing Madison was
teasing the audience with her pelvis.

Inside I let my eyes adjust to the black light. There was
a sudden jerk to my right. In the dark spot reached only by
nipples of electronic light, a lap dancer, a new girl, was strad-
dling a man who smiled leeringly at her, his white teeth glowing.
She needed extra money and would let the men put their cocks

inside of her. With his hands on her hips the man manipulated her body, up and down. She swayed back from him, as if he'd just said something rude.

Drag queens danced on the bar in miniskirts and floppy hats. Madison was dancing topless, wearing denim short-shorts. She had greased her body so it gleamed under the bluish light. The lap dancers wore garters and push-up bras, the men in rumpled business suits, some in cotton sweaters and polyester pants hiked over their bellies. There was a man in a devil mask with a bow tie that squirted water. A woman passed me with a huge extension wig and another in diamond-studded glasses. Lita, the early evening bartender, was grumpy, hated the jump-suit Madison forced her to wear. She said a drunk man had pinched her tit and whenever she reached into the cooler for a frosted glass, it hurt.

I started washing the backed-up glasses, helped Lita pour beers, all the time watching Madison pulse her hips toward the ceiling. I was busy cracking beers, taking money. When I looked up again she was gone and I imagined her on the back stairs, getting a drink of water, putting on her white robe.

But then she was near me, leaning out of the stairwell shouting that she wanted to talk in the bathroom. I followed her. Everyone was drunker than usual and it was a relief to step out of the noise and laughter into the quiet. She locked the door, put down the toilet seat and sat. I hadn't noticed how red the walls were and how people had scratched things into the paint—the letters reminded me of little bones . . . NIGGERS ARE BETTER LOVERS, PUSSY IS GOD. Someone knocked on the door,

Madison ignored it. I noticed through her damp make-up that she looked tired. Pubic hair had gathered on the damp porcelain and someone had left her black bikini underwear rolled up in the corner.

She rubbed the track marks on her arms and tipped her head back, as if wanting the play of colored lights on the underside of her eyelids. I was amazed how she could go for days without sleep. How when she was hurt you could tell only by the movement of her hands. She had no one, so no restrictions either. She couldn't understand worrying about not having a boyfriend or a husband or a baby. Where was her weak spot? Did Pig teach her one person could love another blindly? Or had Pig disappointed her, shown how everyone who loves you needs to control you. Madison thinks that to devastate yourself is somehow life-affirming. I was reminded of a tar-covered cat, a pretty lizard that can shed multiple skins. She looked at me then.

"Susan's not here. Want to make some real money?"

I nodded. Madison stood, opened the door. We entered the noisy bar full of men's faces, numerous and similar as kidney beans. "It will be a relief," she said. "Kneel down to it."

FROM INSIDE SUSAN'S ROOM I COULD HEAR THE FISH TANKS bubbling and men's footfalls in the hall. The room had the glowing muted tones of a baroque painting, with its gold glass lamps and orange satin spread. The black garter belt and stockings were in the closet as Madison had said. I secured the garter

over my hips and affixed each strap to the top of the stocking.
I cracked the seal on the Wild Turkey and swigged directly from
its lip, convincing myself I was waiting for my husband, who was
coming up the stairs in his black banker shoes, locking up our
house. His footsteps creaked on our wood floors, then padded
on the carpeted stairs. He would talk to me while he undressed,
say, "I think we should get some tulip bulbs for the garden."
I'd hear his hangers cling in the closet as he hung up his pants,
then the rich smell of his body coming toward me.

There was a tentative knock, the kind a doctor makes to
see if you've used the paper gown to cover up. I said, "Come
in." He was as old as my father, hair combed over his bald spot
like a gym teacher, his features ragged and pointed like an
eagle's. I started to pull off my clothes and he came over, sat on
the other side of the bed and undressed. When I asked him what
he wanted he said tersely, "To have sex."

I heard him rip the condom package and that sticky
elastic sound as he rolled it down. He turned toward me quickly
and threw one leg over, burying his face in my neck. He forced
his cock in and began a series of anxious little thrusts. There was
a print of a princess with a pale pinched face above the bed. I
noticed how his underarms stank and the ridiculous way he held
his mouth pinched up like a rectum. Both his stench and his
expression reminded me of the professor I had slept with in
college.

The long hairs flapped from his bald head, swayed over
my face. He warned me he was going to come and when he did
his back arched and he moaned. Relaxing his body weight on

top of me, he sucked air for a while, then rolled away, pulled his condom off and lobbed it into the trash can. While he was dressing he watched me with an expression of hate and lust. I leaned back against the headboard, watched him leave, felt the skin of my vagina tingle. I stared at the bulbous lamp on the nightstand, something seemed to be inside of the gold brass waiting to get out. It was an ugly lamp with a faux-suede shade. I thought of how the Nazis had made lamp shades out of people's skin.

The door opened again, slowly, as if the next man hoped to catch me fucking the first. This one was chubby with a little black beard.

"Put your butt up high," he said, closing the door behind him. I got on all fours, cradled my head in my arms, and raised my ass. He unlatched his belt, then his fly, his pants rustled to the floor. Kneeling on the bed in back of me, "Up higher," he said and pressed his cock in, dug his fingernails into my ass. After several long breathy strokes he said, "My brother is going to come in here and put his dick in your mouth, he'll pull your hair until his cock is in to the hilt and you'll moan.

"Moan," he said, and I did. "We'll fuck you every day because you have a nice tight pussy and you liked to be fucked in the ass." He pulled hard and told me he could kill me if he wanted, that nobody would care. I felt his loose tummy resting on my lower back like a rat. His pace accelerated and he made a sound like clearing his throat as he came. He tried to lean over me, to grab my tits, but I jumped away and went into the bathroom, wet a washcloth and wiped my pussy. I looked at the bright sink, the water gurgling in the toilet, the fringe of a towel hanging on a rack by the door. With my hands I pulled my hair straight back and looked into my eyes. *I am still myself.* I remembered after the abortion in college going to a blind shrink, how he held my hand, put his fingers around my wrist. "You're thin," he said. "Is that a problem?" I liked how his one eye was yellowish and glowed like a moon. "You are a girl who has been lonely," he said. "Why do you choose that dark path?"

Madison came in, went over to the bed and poured bourbon into a glass. I put my bell-bottoms on, buttoned my studded shirt. "So was it horrible?" she asked. It was a question similar to the kind my father used to ask when he first left my mother. "Are you O.K.?" he would ask and the only answer would be yes. "It's hard the first few times," she said handing the glass to me. "They haunt you like one-night stands, but if you just relax, it happens. It gets to be like passing people on the street."

"It wasn't really that bad," I said. And it seemed true. Watching the skinhead beating was more riveting and I cried the time my mother called me a bitch. This feeling was so familiar, what happened to me was never real. Emotional experiences happened to others. I got the picture in my head of my mother, brooding, dangerous. And me leaning toward her, caught up in the aura of her pain.

"So now you know what it's like to do the thing most repulsive to women." She took two hundred dollars from her pocket and passed it to me. I started to talk . . . how good it would be to make a lot of money. How I would get my own apartment and a car so we could drive down Highway 1 to L.A.

Madison's cheeks flushed, she looked into her glass. "It's not about money, it's about death."

"Of course it is," I said. "I know that." I was quiet, thinking it over. The glitter in her hair caught light and for a moment there in the half light she looked demonic.

She asked if I'd seen Pig.

"Not since I started," I told her.

Madison wound the top of the bottle down. "I met Pig at a titty bar south of Market. If I let her touch my tits she would give me twenty dollars. Eventually she offered to pay me to come over and walk up and down her spine."

"Then you lived with her?"

"Only after she begged me. I was a lap dancer and lived with a guy who sculpted naked ladies. He got hooked on heroin and started stealing from me. I holed up at Pig's. It wasn't so bad until she started to get that look whenever I went near her. One night she was looking at me." Madison burlesqued Pig's dreamy eyes. "And I realized if I slept with her, she would think of it forever. So I did her and it was O.K., till she started moaning."

Madison laughed. I knew I should too, but her attitude toward Pig was cruel and adolescent. It was one thing to say Pig had taken advantage of her, another to make fun of her sexuality. She doubled over laughing. I felt uncomfortable and watched the street light move on the curtains. Madison was acting crazy, but I didn't trust my observations because the chair ribs hurt my back and the rug was rough on my bare feet. My bourbon looked like a flame—*I have done the thing I was most afraid of . . . what will happen now?*

AFTER WORK MADISON TOOK ME TO A PLACE IN CHINATOWN JUST off Grant Street called the Buddah Bar. High black-vinyl stools and a sagging string of blinking paper lanterns lined the bar. When the bartender saw Madison he nodded hello and hit a little brass bell attached to the cash register. A slim woman appeared in an electrician's jumpsuit wearing round wire frames with rose-colored glass. She led us silently down the back stairs and along a narrow hallway to a metal door fortified by several dead-bolt locks. I swayed woozily . . . time no longer held me. I felt lucky, freed, as I had been, by a fifth of bourbon. I watched a vein in Madison's temple pulse, stepped back so I could mouth, without her seeing me, "She is wild . . . she is dangerous." Madison pounded the door with the side of her fist.

"Open up," she said. "It's me." The eyehole darkened and then a melodious voice, I thought at first it came from inside my drunken head, said . . . "Madison dear, hold on." The tone was deep, but slightly tilted like a woman's. Keys jangled and the first of many locks clicked back.

"Habee is a hermaphrodite," Madison whispered. "If you're nice to him he may show you." She licked her fingers and smoothed her eyebrows. The door opened and there was Habee, a Lebanese man in coffee-colored silk pajamas, his long hair held in a braid down his back. He had small breasts like a teenager and was deeply tan like people who live out-of-doors.

"Delighted," Habee said, swinging his hands open and kissing Madison. "If Madison hasn't told you," he said, turning to me, "this is where it all leaves off."

"This is a friend of mine," she said as we stepped inside. "Isn't she lovely?"

Habee held my chin between his thumb and forefinger, forced my head to the left for a profile. Then took my hands, turned them over and back. He shook his head.

"I haven't seen anything like her since I was in Amsterdam." He led us to one of the low tables in the middle of the room. Sweet smoke hung near the ceiling, the walls were tiled in mosque patterns of blues and greens, and maroon Orientals covered the floors. Four high standing candelabras gave the place plenty of light. No hard furniture to sit on, just pillows and several short wooden tables for hookah pipes. There were shadows behind the drapes dividing the room into private compartments and a soft smell of sweat. A man in a tuxedo was lying down with his hand propping up his head. His hair was slick and black and when he sat up to greet me, he kissed my hand.

"Better to search for heaven than not," he said.

"Oh loosen up," Habee said. "You're behaving all wrong." The man got up, bowed, put one arm over his head and the other elegantly out to the side and tiny-stepped on his tiptoes away from us toward another group of people talking near the gold tile fireplace on the far side of the room.

"What'sa matter with Georgie?" Madison said.

"Oh, you know, he doesn't really like girls."

"I do," she said, pressing her shoulder against mine. I

could tell she was glad I was here. She'd matched me shot for shot at Carmen's, but had gotten only more dignified . . . more prophetic. She'd told me I'd eventually regret every night of my life except for this one. And with the bourbon surrounding everything with a lovely halo of melancholy, I thought, *She is so right.*

Habee lit the opium in the glass bottom of the hookah pipe and the perfumed smoke wafted toward me.

"I must tell you both," Habee said, taking short puffs to keep the smoke coming, "about a trip I just took to Mexico. I went to see an old friend of mine. I had no idea it would be so fantastic. He and about twenty others stay in caves by the water. All day they swim and fuck. A woman brings their food. They just stretch out in the sun like otters, it was the most remarkable thing."

"Sounds like you found your calling," Madison said, accepting the pipe, adjusting the hose so the smoke could move easily into her mouth.

"No, my best times were in the circus. I had a lovely gown . . . silk with blue roses. And there was a boy who gave me flowers. Really, he got quite obsessed with me and would wait until late to walk me to my trailer." Habee took the pipe himself, puffed a thoughtful pigeon of smoke. "Anyway, it had to do with a rainy day and a back rub."

"Sounds lurid," I said, taking the mouthpiece and putting it to my lips. The smoke was smooth as milk.

"Yes?" Habee said, opening his eyes wide and waiting.

"Well." I exhaled. "Did you hurt him?"

Habee smiled and took the pipe. "I assure you I did not. But that reminds me of a theory I'm developing. I think if men still hunted for deer or bear, more of them would be happy with their wives. Because now, you see, all men can hunt is women. It's terrible for them, their last connection to that savage wild man. They hunt. They kill."

"Kill?" Madison said.

"You know, the moment a man comes, he's taken what he needs to feed himself."

I felt queasy about his theory and about the little boy. I felt confused. I knew adultery was O.K., as was homosexuality and prostitution, but what about incest and older people taking advantage of younger ones? What about murder and cannibalism? It all made me uneasy because I could foresee being able to understand almost anything. I knew extreme behavior—hate, lust, domination—could be, as in Madison's case, just an extreme type of self-preservation. And I knew too that Habee would agree with Madison, that it was a weak and herdish thing to be "good." Being nice was just a cover for weakness. I knew too that I was capable of knowing what was good for me, but doing the opposite. Once while I was home on Christmas break from school I slept with an old lover in some strange house he had the keys to. The sheets smelled like other people's bodies. My lover was melancholy, drank beers, brooded. It made me feel uneasy, even now, because I'd known it wasn't right to go there every evening to fuck and smoke cigarettes in a stranger's bed, but I did it anyway.

Everything around me seemed suddenly lushly alive. The

ceramic patterns on the walls looked like DNA chains. Madison was talking about a john who had only wanted to kiss. "And he kissed so fake," she said, "like he thought he was a movie star."

She turned to me and put her lips on mine, opened her mouth and let her tongue wiggle around. Her mouth tasted of melon and I felt as if I were swimming in very warm water.

"The two of you are wonderful to behold," Habee said, patting his heart.

Madison laughed and started to tell about a time when she was little. She'd forced all the kids in her neighborhood to take communion: wine made from poison sumac berries.

Had she really wanted to kiss me or was she showing off for Habee? Even her most intimate gestures were ambiguous. She was listening to him talk now about his mother, how she never woke, sleeping with her hands palsied up and the pee trickling into the clear plastic bag beside her. "It is a shame," he said, "that such a precious spirit has taken flight." Then Madison told about her mother, how she'd been raped and murdered in a lot behind the local grocery store, how the guy poured lighter fluid over her and set the whole field on fire.

"Jesus," I said. "You don't just tell a story like that."

They both looked at me, surprised the story startled me. Habee patted me coldly, turned to Madison, who told how the police had searched for the man though he was never found. Watching Madison talk I realized her coldness and cruelty were ways, known only to herself, of feeling more strongly than others.

Shadows shifted again behind the silk divider near us. A

man breathed rhythmically and I could see a pelvis swaying against the rear and back of a bent figure. The sound of skin slapping skin reminded me of the skinheads. Madison touched my arm and said, "He's agreed to show you." Habee was waiting, with his fingers splitting his pajamas, showing me his cunt, which was wide and lovely with folds and folds of pink skin. From inside came the limp cock, tiny balls too. I thought strangely of my mother, how she walked around the house in a half-slip, how she showed me rashes on her thighs, a pimple on her breast, how there seemed no delineation between her pain and mine. I asked, "Does any of it work?" He leaned toward me, his strong smell of cinnamon and the sweet smoke of opium swirled and he said, "It all depends on what you mean."

Chapter

Eight

IT WAS NEARLY DAWN. THE TRAFFIC LIGHT'S REDS, YELLOWS AND greens were magic in the blue half light. We left Habee's and walked through Chinatown. Madison stopped to chat with the live chickens in the cage of the poultry store, then pointed at a jade display of lovers in a variety of sexual positions. We were headed for a diner in the Tenderloin that Madison said had the best marmalade toast in San Francisco. My body felt light and the littlest details were miraculous: the store window with a row of old man's hats, the elegant way Madison flung her cigarette. The lightening sky reminded me of when I was young, before I knew the difference between living things and dead ones.

The diner was classic, white tile with Art Deco aluminum details. A sign written in longhand advertised the breakfast specials. Madison pulled the door open. Her exhaustion manifested itself as speedy strength. We took a booth near the front windows. There were a couple of drag queens at the counter eating pie and a black man two booths down with a little white mutt on his lap. I'd seen him around on his bike carrying the dog in the front basket. The waitress slapped down the plastic-covered menus, stood with her pen poised over her pad. She was thin like a boy, her netted hair resting on her head like a crown.

"Two breakfast specials," Madison said, lighting another cigarette, "with extra jam."

"How do you want your eggs?" the waitress asked.

"Over easy," she said and the drag queens laughed.

She drank one cup of coffee after another, looking out the window at the steam rising from a manhole cover. I inhaled her smoke, watched the shoulders of the Mexican fry-cook stooping over the grill. She was like a man in her insistence on quiet camaraderie. Madison sipped her coffee, opened another small plastic container of cream, three more packets of sugar. There was pain in her face, but it was hard to tell if it was for her mother. It was horrible to imagine her mother, vulnerable in a flimsy flowered housedress, dragged behind the grocery store. Madison arranged her life so she'd be close to her mother, close to death. The waitress set the plates down roughly. My eggs were runny. The yokes reminded me of body fluids and the bacon scent was nauseating. I pushed my plate away. Madison cut her egg whites with her fork into splinters, then reached one up tentatively to her mouth. She concentrated entirely on eating, swallowing firmly. She sniffed her toast, emptied two containers of marmalade on the slices and took a bite. The sun was there now, pink on the flesh-tone buildings across the street. A bald man came in with a lunch bag and a newspaper.

"Is that story about your mother true?" My nerves were wasted and it upset me so much to ask that my hand trembled on the coffee cup. She seemed angry.

"I used to be like you. I went around sticking my nose in everyone's business, thinking I was a garbage pail for everyone's misery. Everything seemed so sad, too sad to bear."

"You think compassion is a malady?"

"Everybody does," Madison said. "Now I just try to forget myself by forcing my body into extreme situations. You may think I'm a fool, but it's the way I saved myself."

"Did you ever ask someone for help?" I hated myself, I sounded like a goddamn television commercial.

"You mean God?" She laughed. "I know I should make peace with my past, but I can't. Therapy is for people like you, who have little problems, like divorced parents or husbands who can't get it up."

"I don't know," I said. "I think people can help each other."

"Well, you probably believe in democracy too." She lifted her yolk onto her toast.

The coffee was hitting my nerves hard. I wanted her to stay with me. I suddenly felt horribly lonely. "What I meant was, I want to help you."

"I can't stomach this," she said, throwing down her fork. "Why can't you just sit there quietly and watch me eat?"

I HURRIED BACK TO THE APARTMENT, LAY DOWN ON THE BED and pretended to be dead. I fell off quickly, had dreams of the dead, vivid and horrible. I opened my mouth and lizards came out. I dreamt I was walking naked in the Tenderloin with a baby made of cheese and another the size of a matchstick. To make the small one grow, I put it in warm water, but it turned blue. I tried to breast-feed it, and at first, it was amazing: the milk, the baby's adorable little mouth, but then it turned into a thick black catfish with long insect antennae. A man spoke Spanish in the next room, his voice rose until he was screaming and I opened my eyes and realized it was the phone ringing.

"Finally," my mother said, when I picked up. "Where have you been?"

"I started a new job last night."

"Waitressing?" she asked.

"Yeah," I lied.

"Make lots of money?"

"Yep," I said.

"Good," she said. "Maybe you can get yourself some new clothes." I cradled the phone to my shoulder and shut the curtain against the growing morning light. "I called you because of these incredible stories I heard at a party last night. Remember Timmy Rollins? He dropped out of college and started working as night janitor at the big insurance building on the highway? Last week when he found his girlfriend with another man, he broke her jaw and pulled out half the hair on her head."

"Jesus!" I said.

"And do you remember June?"

"The one with the fluffy sweaters?"

"That's right. Well, she was cleaning up her VCR unit and noticed an unfamiliar tape, so she popped it in, and there was her husband having sex with a young woman."

"No way," I said, imagining the wife in her robe watching her husband with a woman much like herself, only ten years younger. The TV screen buzzing.

"I'll tell you," my mother went on, "someone should write a book on man's true character."

"Is that girl Timmy beat up O.K.?" I asked.

"You only get one chance in life, and for women that chance comes early. Before you know it, the million-dollar-baby thing is gone." I didn't answer. It made me angry that she hated men yet sometimes sided with them. She wanted to believe, even though Dad had left her, that the patriarchy would care for her.

I was thinking of Madison, realizing she was similar to my mother, both believed that hate was sustaining. They each had a well-developed sense of doom and were convinced it was unresolvable, convinced the only way to lessen their pain was to pass it on to others.

"Do you ever pretend that you're dead?" I asked her.

"Jesse, why would you ask me something so morbid?"

"Because I'm exhausted," I said.

She harrumphed. "You only have one mother."

"And I only have one life."

"You call playing house a life?"

"I'll call you," I said.

"Do you have to go?" she asked.

"Yes," I said and hung up.

When I thought of the expensive tailored clothes she'd worn as a teenager, still kept in plastic in her dresser, or of the TV show about a career woman she'd watched faithfully when we were little kids, I felt a searing empathy. But on the phone her semiotic stories always carried a curse for me and it was all I could do to protect myself. Too, I felt responsible, still, that Dad had dumped her, mostly because it was hard to pretend that she, or anyone really, was easy to love.

I rolled over on my stomach, moved my arms just under my hip bones, and cupped my palms over my pussy—it was a position I had used since I was a baby. Through the bed I heard the voice of a Chinese woman below and, above, the footfalls of the lovers rising, the woman's fluttering feet in the kitchen, the man in the shower. I imagined my mother coming to me. She lay over me, and started to pulse her pelvis. There was something so familiar about giving her pleasure, something I'd been trying to do all of my life.

THE NEXT NIGHT I WENT IN THROUGH THE BACK DOOR AT Carmen's, saw Madison waiting at the top of the stairs. The stairwell was dimly lit and I liked the priestly way she stood, wearing the same clothes as last night. As I got closer I could tell she was high.

"The snake beguiled me and I ate," she said. I felt uncomfortable. Whenever time lapsed, she seemed to forget the status of our relationship. "I have a hardcore upstairs," she said, somewhat bored. "He likes an audience."

"I just watch?"

Madison nodded.

"O.K." I followed, her scent rich like menstrual blood. I was curious, I still hadn't felt that exquisite kick of perversity. A man sat on the bed—he was younger than I had imagined, with pale blond hair and small perverse features. In his bow tie and expensive suit, he looked awkward as a game bird in Madison's space-age room.

"I thought I told you to undress," Madison said, not looking at the man as she poured me an inch of bourbon in a blue glass.

The man slipped off his shoe, then pulled his sock off and folded it into the loafer. He removed his other shoe, rolled the sock down, placed that sock inside of the other shoe. His hands shook as he put both shoes together next to the bed. He unzipped his pants, stepped out one leg at a time, folded them neatly and placed the pants on top of his shoes. Then he undid his bow tie and took off his shirt, till he stood in his flowered boxers, shivering, looking anxious and pleased.

"Those too," Madison said firmly. He pulled them down, folded the boxers on the top of his pile. His skin goose-pimpled and he looked at her longingly, waiting for directions.

"Bend over the bed," she ordered.

He draped himself over the edge. Cracked his butt so I

could see his anus, dark pubic hair curling around it. I slung down the bourbon, my organs glowing like a space heater. Was this Madison's idea of intimacy, me staring into this guy's asshole?

She sat down at her dressing table, got out a fingernail clipper and snapped the white nail from her thumb. The man gasped. Madison worked on the other hand, with each snap of a fingernail the man moaned. She took off a go-go boot, folded her foot up onto the chair and clipped her toenails.

"This woman here," she said, "is going to tell your little boys all about you."

I winced. Though the man didn't say anything I could tell she'd excited him. Now that I knew something about her past, Madison was no less of an enigma. She wanted to escape her own consciousness in another's flesh, but it made me uncomfortable that it wasn't sex she considered exciting, but the idea of evil. Madison preferred the narrative, the "then I do this" to the reality. She considered the sexual narrative holy and could thus disentangle herself from the act.

She took off her other boot, a deep click for the thick nail of her big toe and then smaller snaps as she cut the nails in decreasing size. She put each boot back on and zipped them up. She opened a drawer and took out a rubber glove. Pulled it up over her hand and snapped it at her elbow. She took up a tube of lubricating jelly and squeezed some over the glove, spreading it out so the rubber gleamed. She straightened two fingers and squeezed a drop out onto the tip. When the man heard her stand he sighed and spread his cheeks further. I could see his hard cock peeking out between his stomach and the bed.

Madison sat next to him and slid two fingers slowly into his anus. She slipped in a third finger, moved them in to the hilt. The man's legs jangled softly. With a continual slow movement back and forth she pushed her whole hand in, then her wrist, her forearm. She fisted her hand and the man sucked air. His back arched, his pink anus was stretched wide as a mouth. Madison moved her arm in and out, she seemed fascinated by the way the rubber glove disappeared inside the man's asshole. She punched up hard, the man raised his head, gasped. Her arm in to the elbow, she flexed her bicep and grabbed for his bowels. The man made a series of vowel sounds. Then a hard "Hhhhhhhhhh" that rose high like a cat's scream. Madison's lips opened into a snarl and I could see the muscles of her neck strain and flex. He splayed his arms and legs wildly like a bug with a pin through its belly.

"Madison," I yelled instinctually. She looked at me, but her eyes were dead. She had gone away from me, away from the man, the room and Carmen's, away from San Francisco too. Madison was on the lot behind the grocery store watching the flames. She quickly looked back down, reached around the man to restrain him with a tight arm around his waist. She knew fathers didn't have to be loving toward their children, that mothers could be raped like schoolgirls, that people's relationships to one another are sinister, violent, even murderous. He wailed, his eyes bulged and he swung his head side to side.

"Madison," I yelled again, but she was concentrating now, reaching her fingers up toward his heart. *She wants his heart,* I thought, *because she doesn't have one of her own.* I ran out of the room, down the back stairs and onto the street.

I WAS HEADED FOR THE BLACK ROSE TO FIND BELL. WATCHING Madison's fist made me realize Bell had never treated me like a lover. He lived with me to appease his dead father and I stayed with him because his loving disinterest was exactly the kind of mixed signal I used to get from my mother. I wondered if Bell missed me. I'll tell him how I whored myself because he rejected my body—not just its surface, but its general longing. I'll tell him that there is more strength in low moments than in powerful ones. "Bell," I will say, "there is something centering about despair." But he would be disappointed that I had left Madison's, say I was fascist to think that heterosexual sex was the only cosmically right kind, that whenever one body enters another it was life-affirming.

Bell sat in the corner of the Black Rose in a red leather booth. He seemed different, with his dirty hair parted to the side and the lining of his coat ripped so it hung down like a rag. He looked up, grabbed my hand and kissed the palm deeply.

"I convinced myself that you were dead," he said, pulling me across the table to him. He smelled of stale smoke and beerish sweat. "You must come back."

I pulled away and sat back. "I can't do that."

"You don't understand." He looked into my eyes, his skin was liverish, puffy. "I'm afraid I'm going crazy."

I shook my head. "I came here to tell you that the only reason we were together was because you thought your father would have loved me." He hardly listened.

"Oh Jesse, things are so much worse than that. I can't sleep. I feel like somebody will trick me if I do, all I can think of is my poor father. I was just remembering how I promised to take him to the theater. He came up because it was my first long-running show. We were supposed to meet at two o'clock and I got there a little early, sat across the street to wait, drank a beer in a diner. He showed up, stood out front. I watched him. He looked ridiculous with his thick arms and striped rugby shirt. I thought he was too excited and I would be embarrassed. He tried the locked theater door several times. The horrible thing is that I took pleasure in this."

"It certainly wasn't very nice, but you can't do anything about it now," I said. "He's dead."

Bell shook his head. "But he was always so kind to me and I did horrible things. On Father's Day we had a special breakfast. Mom bought a coffee cake and she forced me to get a present. He was thrilled, touched my arm, then opened the box to find an old stained tie that I found in the neighbor's garbage. My father put on the tie, smiled, kissed me and finished his breakfast."

"Bell," I said, "stop torturing yourself."

"I can't, I just keep thinking of incidents that make me writhe." He looked into his gin and began to fold his napkin into smaller and smaller squares. The bartender brushed near us with a wrapped grocery-store log and placed it on the fire. It didn't give off any heat, but the flames were green and purple like a bruise.

"When he died I saw a demon, furred, batlike, crawl out of his mouth." Bell's eyes closed and tears dripped through his lashes down his cheek.

I put my hand over his, squeezed. He opened his wet eyes and said, "You don't understand how I'm already in hell." He stood and walked back to the bathroom.

A man at the bar stared at me. He had a full face and wore a leather jacket that tightened at his wrists with zippers. He narrowed his eyes on me. I got nervous thinking he was a customer at Carmen's. I was almost sure not. There was something appealing about him that told me he didn't pay for sex.

The man walked over. "So," he said, and it was the humid hot house smell and his fat calloused fingers that made me realize it was the stranger from Madison's room.

Bell walked up, took his seat in the booth. "Friend of yours?" he asked.

I couldn't think of anything to say and besides all the air in the place seemed to be gone. "Please go," I said stiffly.

"Why you working this faggot?" the stranger said.

"What?" Bell's face reddened as he looked from the man to me. The stranger took a swig from my glass. Bell rose up off the bench, but the stranger pushed him back into the booth.

"You see," he said, "it's my job to tell little fags like you the secrets about their girlfriends."

"What's the truth about you?" Bell asked. "That you try to get girls off the school bus, that you have herpes, that you fucked your mother?"

"You little fuck." He grabbed Bell, pulled him from the booth, moved him over to the exposed brick wall and raised his arm. Bell's eyes bulged. The bartender's voice was loud. "No goddamn fights in the Rose." Then he was on the stranger, pulling him back, telling him to act civilly or he'd kick his butt out onto the street.

Bell was upset, he told me he'd wait outside and walked swiftly to the door.

I watched the stranger as he glared at the bartender walking back to the bar. "Did Madison tell you I was waiting in her room?" I asked.

The stranger nodded, grabbed my wrist. "Have that door open," he said. "I'll be coming around."

WHEN BELL SAW ME COME OUT OF THE BLACK ROSE HE TURNED his head. He was waiting in a doorway, smoking a cigarette. Everything was horrible, but it had always been like that, and I felt relieved, the pressure to keep things *nice* was gone. When I came near, he dropped his cigarette and crushed it with his shoe.

"I won't be able to think of anything else but your delicate hips fucking that thing."

Nervously, I fingered the lapel of his coat. "It's easier than thinking of us together in some sort of regular life."

He didn't answer and we stood in dry silence. I remembered a day we'd walked to the pond with the swans in Golden Gate Park, how he'd touched my hair as the birds rose and I looked up into his face.

Chapter
Nine

I PASSED THE TATTOO MUSEUM, SEXPLOSION AND THE LUSTY Lady. On the corner of Eddy and Taylor a man in a wheel-chair was peddling paper roses that lit up in the middle. And a little farther up a man in a jogging suit, holding a baby on his shoulders, tried to sell me a bus transfer. The strong wind blew trash around the street and there was a skinny junkie in corduroy bell-bottoms smoking crack in a doorway. I ducked into an Arabian deli and bought a quart of beer, stood in front of the porno-video shop looking at the blue lava lamps in Carmen's upper windows. I drank recklessly thinking it would excite the men talking out front. It felt right drinking beer, one eye on the lava lamps and the other on the soft-porn movie playing on the screen in the window. I looked for my reflection, but there wasn't any. Chilly, I pulled my shirt sleeves over my wrists. It didn't really surprise me that Madison had the stranger fuck me. She didn't believe in equality, she manipulated me like a slave. Her philosophy was seductively dangerous.

I'd taken my parents too literally, because it was clear now I wasn't a princess. My emotions were complicated, but no better than the whores' at Carmen's. Liars attracted me because I was one myself. I was like all women who have great fidelity to their memories and delusions.

The empty quart made a hollow scratchy sound as I set it against the brick wall. I went in the back door of Carmen's, up the dim stairway. The fishtanks seemed louder than usual and the black light made the white shag purple. Between blasts of strobe light Susan danced in her window. I walked straight up the spiral steps into Madison's room. She sat at her dressing table with her head tipped forward. At first I thought she was praying, but then I saw the syringe and rubber tube behind her. She was asleep and I walked closer, saw that the roots of her splayed hair were dirty blond and how the veins of her arm were bruised. She lifted her head and I stepped back.

"I can always tell when someone is watching me," she said.

"I ran into the guy you sent over to fuck me."

"And?" Madison sat up, laughed awkwardly.

"Fuck you, Madison! You might as well have raped me yourself."

"What's the big deal? You're already past your prime,

every man you fuck has and is going to fuck someone else."

It took all my willpower not to hit her. "I can't believe you think being a whore helps."

"It helps me," she said, flopping onto the bed.

"You're sick," I said.

"Meaningful relationships flutter between two things, convention and sentimentality."

"Some stranger can't mean more than a lover or someone in your family."

"That's the point . . . they do to *God* and they do to me . . . This is silly," she said. "Come over here. Do you want me to say you *mean* something to me?"

When I didn't answer she said, "You're so predictable." She unbuttoned her shirt, showed me her pale cleavage, her hard pierced nipples. "I'll touch you with an incident from my sad sad childhood, how my father raped me, how my mother was murdered . . . then maybe you'll kiss me." She pulled her blouse off one shoulder and her breasts goose-pimpled. "You want your life to be like a movie," she said. "That's why you won't come to me . . . because it's not perfect enough. For you, everything is ruined before it even begins. Do you want me to tell you I love you?" she said.

I still wouldn't come to her and this made her angry, she clicked her jaw.

"You'll see," she said. "Relationships are like wallpaper patterns, you think you're moving forward but you're always caught in your own obsessions."

"You are already dead," I said to her. It hadn't been what I intended to say, but it seemed true enough.

She jumped up from the bed and flew at me, chased me down the stairs. "I know what you're thinking!" she screamed. "Get out of here with all your true-love bullshit!"

PIG SAT IN THE LIVING ROOM ON THE CRIMSON VICTORIAN, tarot cards spread out over the marble coffee table. She looked very put together in her huge gabardine suit and pinkish wig. Her bracelets jingled.

"I absolutely knew in my heart of hearts you'd return." She patted the sofa near her signaling for me to sit down. Pig's body heat was like a radiator. I leaned into her and she put her arm around me. "You just can't wear your heart on your sleeve dear," Pig said, "unless you have big teeth. Not everyone is as good as you at falling in love." She pressed my head into her breast and smoothed down my hair. "I knew a man once, met him in a café reading working-class poetry. He had these dreamy bedroom eyes. He told me right away that his mother had died lately of a heart attack, that he'd once accidentally killed a man with his car and that his girlfriend was a whore. His pupils were dilated and I saw the raised keloid scars on his wrists. He carried his red wine over to my table and told me that a little boy had found a dead baby in the woods. The boy thought it was an angel because clenched in its stiff blue hand was a white feather. What I'm saying," Pig said, "is that horror is everywhere, it's the rule, not the exception. Life is a disease." Pig paused, her breath smelled of wintergreen, she swung her fat leg gently but it knocked the coffee table. "After so many broken hearts, the really bloody kind—I've decided it's better to rely on memories. I sift mine, refine them, till they are like jewels in a black velvet bag."

I pulled away from her. "That makes them lies."

Pig was creepy. Her emotional reflexes were mild, unfocused, so she relied on emotions of the past.

Pig looked up at me, startled. "You think I'm a liar?" There was a long silence, the kind when you run out of things to say or get caught off guard. When she did speak it was slow, and she didn't look at me. "Pity is such a strange emotion. Once felt, disgust is never far off and then too a certain need to make it perfectly clear the pitied is completely separate from the pitier. This is done mostly with moralistic accusations of the sort you just used on me. This pedanticism," she said loudly and stamped her foot. "I'll tell you something. I stayed with a man in my mother's summer house and never changed the sheets. To my mother it meant I didn't love her, and that my men were more important than her." Pig sipped her wine. "Of course, she was right. Sex is a kind of alchemy. It's the one thing other than death that if used properly can change everything, like that first night with Madison, it's all in my head like a beautiful dream. I remember her skin. Its texture made me believe I'd never die." She looked out the window over the mud range behind the house.

I had no sympathy for Pig's rambling lyricism, because I felt like a rat in a garbage can. There would never be peace. My

father, in leaving my mother, poisoned my memories of childhood. That's why Madison's idea that family members had no
ordained purpose one to another appealed to me. My family
splintered as if they'd been together for the shooting of a movie.

I was glad I'd pitched my polluted self into Bell's memory, because he confused his urge to please his dying father with
passion for me. Our relationship, like all romantic ones, had
been fodder for the family.

"Madison is a whore," I said. "And so am I."

The color drained from Pig's face. "So," she nodded.
Her face falling in on itself.

"Did you expect she was married with a baby in some
split-level ranch?"

She looked into my eyes, at my hands, the set of my
shoulders, tried to figure out why I'd sabotaged her memory of
Madison. Pig shook her monstrous legs and leaned forward to
rise.

"Get me my coat," she said. "We are going out."

IN THE TAXI PIG PRETENDED NOT TO BE SURPRISED BY THE LACK
of neighboring houses, by the mud lots stretching all the way to
the water. Though I saw her flinch as we passed a man in a gray
hooded sweatshirt laid out on a dirty mattress. Closer to Carmen's the skyscrapers pressing up to the cab and the taxis' hectic
movements seemed to frighten Pig. She tried to make small talk
with the cabbie: Latin music, how seductive it was, how fla-
menco was the most sensuous of dances. But he just nodded

and looked into his rearview mirror as if he didn't understand English. On Polk Street Pig pointed out the window, her mouth open. "Isn't that Bell?"

It was him, standing near the Black Rose in his dirty overcoat talking to a strange young man.

"Who's that with him?" She touched my arm.

"I don't know," I said and twisted my body toward the door: I did not want to talk about Bell.

At Carmen's I paid and helped Pig out of the backseat. Her eyes still hadn't adjusted to outside light and she was unsure of her footing and squinted as we walked to the door. Inside, she seemed to relax immediately: the darkness, the rows and rows of booze. We took stools at the bar. It was early so the place was empty. The lap dancers drank at the other end and the disco music was superfluous like Christmas decorations after the new year. We ordered red wine and she smiled when she saw the tall thin glass. We didn't speak for a while, she was busy absorbing the decor: black-light murals, the metal bar. I was preoccupied too, trying to decide why I'd agreed to take her here. Wouldn't it only hurt Pig more? Was it evil? I hoped Pig and Madison would turn into me and my mother, that they would say true things to one another. Whenever the front door opened she got edgy.

"What will you say to her?" I asked.

"That I love her," she said. "That's all I want to say." Pig was like a mother in that what she perceived as simple love carried a truckload of complications. "When you love a woman, you love yourself, and it's terrible really, how it seems perfectly possible to swallow the other. With a man you want to join, you want your ribs to connect like handcuffs. But with a woman if you swallow, she becomes you."

"Is Madison the main one," I asked.

"Well, yes and no, there was Claudine, a little black girl from France. She was into a kind of sophisticated drag. Once walking home from a party, she went into an alley to pee and when she walked back, all I could see was her dinner jacket floating toward me."

The lap dancers giggled at the end of the bar. They were wondering who Pig was and why I was with her.

"Do they have children?" Pig asked, motioning to them.

"Some do."

"I think the idea of reproduction is absurd." She felt insecure, but was hiding it behind indignation. What exactly she was thinking I couldn't tell, but it must have pivoted around some derailed idea of motherhood. Maybe her obsession with Madison was shored by a biological yearning.

Pig ordered another glass of wine. Her cheeks flushed and her fat fingers curled around her drink. A little base make-up gathered in the ridges of her nose. "But Madison, she is like nobody else, like a wolf caught in the body of a woman. I'll never forget how once, drunk on sake, very late on a rainy night, the tenth night of hard rain, Madison said it was God beating his fist, that she couldn't take it anymore, and would confess everything to me. She told me how in Paris she'd stuffed her dead baby into a trash can, wrapped in clear plastic. It's name was Elaina and it wore a tiny emerald ring. All that night she was insane, fucked several men then spent the money on drink. Early in the morning she was walking in a quiet neighborhood. The gray stone buildings were damp, water dripped off the black grillwork. Ahead she saw an older lady in a raincoat wearing a funny little felt hat. Madison said what rose in her was a kind of blind rage. This old woman had survived, her very life condemned Madison's. She rushed her, sat on her chest and cut her throat. She stared at the woman, her skirt twisted, her throat cut crudely with a penknife. Madison said the woman's eyes were completely colorless."

"Madison killed someone?" It shouldn't have surprised me, but it did. It was the logical end to everything I knew about Madison, but it was hard to believe, coming from Pig. True or not it tinted every idea or memory of her.

Pig nodded. "So you see, it makes her special in a way." Pig watched the bartender bend over into the cooler. "I still have all her old love letters stored in satin boxes. It upsets me to read them." Pig trailed off, stared past me at Madison, who'd come into the bar from the back stairs. "Honey," Pig called to her, rising up on her stool.

Madison wasn't surprised. "Fat as ever, huh, Pig," she said, walking over.

Pig blushed. "I'd like to speak to you about some things."

Madison nodded O.K. and pointed outside. The intimacy between them surprised me. Madison had a certain respect for Pig. Or maybe in Carmen's Madison treated everyone like a customer. I ordered another drink, thought how people are different things to different people. Maybe this was what I resisted? It upset me that my lovers always had old lovers. I wanted a pureness in my relationships. But Bell longed for Kevin and my father has a new wife. The story of Adam and Eve has less to do with evil than the cosmic human sadness that relationships are never straightforward, never pure enough.

Out the window I could see the glittering sidewalk and Pig crossing her arms over her breasts as Madison lectured her. I thought of all the things I wanted to tell my own mother— that I loved her but wished she wasn't so needy, so depressed, so unhappy. And that I felt responsible for her unhappiness, it was suffocating. Pig put her arm on Madison's shoulder, looking at the ground while she spoke. They resembled each other in a general way as women do who have had a hard life. Madison leaned into Pig, then pulled away and said something surly. Pig shook her head. Their different positions reminded me of various relationships, mother, daughter, sisters, husband and wife. Nobody knew what went on between two people except those two. I thought of Bell and decided to leave. This place was as constant as the planets and I felt even worse knowing that.

They both looked up when the door opened and I told them I was going. Pig urged me to stay but Madison said, "Fuck her, let her go." I turned, realized how sullen my voice sounded. I did feel left out, but it didn't matter. I would never know what was between them, what held them together, what kept them apart. It was impossible as holding a beating heart in your hands.

* * *

THE PHONE WAS RINGING WHEN I GOT HOME AND I KNEW before I answered it that it was my mother.

"Your father," she said as soon as I said hello, "says he's not going to send my checks anymore. He says I'm a leech."

"Maybe he doesn't have it. You can't bleed a stone."

"That's just what he said. You're just like him. I remember the time I found those unopened letters in your dorm room. He used to not open letters from people he didn't care about."

"Mom, we've been through this a hundred times. He's my father."

"But he's evil, I just can't take this anymore. He leaves, you leave. It's like my family's been bombed. It's fine for the strong people, but not for people like me. I'm not very sophisticated." She was quiet and I could tell by the way she took in air that she was trying not to cry. "Lately, I haven't wanted to live."

I resisted her, because of her hard childhood, her alcoholic father. She was often melodramatic, always trying to convince me of an inevitable doom. "I know how you feel," I said.

"Do you?" she said. "Do you really understand? My father was a drunk, he'd forget where he left his car at least once a week. Once he got frostbite because he passed out on the street. Jesse, I married your father because I thought I'd be assured a good life. A minister would provide for me, would be kind and honest. But he cheated and humiliated me," she yelled.

"I can't take this, stuck in this town your father dragged me to. When will he get what he deserves?"

"Mom," I said, "I'm sorry you feel that way."

"I don't need this." She was furious now. "You are an accomplice, you and your father talking about poetry, taking walks, you in a little pair of shorts. I know what he was trying to do and you loved the attention. You loved stealing him from me."

"I was a teenager."

"You hurt me so much," she said. I realized in a clear, more defined way how broken she was. I was angry at myself, that she had to offer me her jugular, like a submissive dog, before I felt anything for her. "God damn it," she shrieked now. "I am so fucking lonely." She never swore and this fact alone more than anything she said upset me. I saw how divorce just cements the patterns of a dysfunctional family, it institutionalizes and canonizes the sickness, assures it a place forever. Compassion streamed in with so much intensity I felt light-headed.

"I'll come home," I said, "if that's what you want."

"I'm sorry," she said. "It's just too much for me."

"Do you want me to come home? I will."

"No," she said. "What good would that do?" She started to cry and told me she had to go, she'd call back later when she was feeling better. "It's not just me, it's everyone," she said and hung up.

I put the receiver down gently. Illuminated by the dirty street light, my room looked dull. It was bare like a hotel room and even the things that marked it—the horny blowfish, the cubist painting, the dead carnations in the vase by the bed—seemed dangerous. I lay down and felt a kind of insipid anxiety that hinted at tomorrow's depression. I closed my eyes, thought, *Jesus and Bell and Kevin.* The wedding invitation rested on the nightstand. It was traditional with raised black letters, a little envelope and small bits of tissue paper. The wedding was in Los Angeles tomorrow at five. I went to the window. A Mexican whore came out of the hotel across the street. Kevin's features came to me.

Chapter

Ten

I WALKED LIGHTLY UP THE STAIRS AND PUT MY EAR TO BELL'S door. If his breath was even, his countenance calm, I'd tell him I was going to Kevin's wedding. The radio was on, a talk show about the chances of war. I could see words scratched into the wood. I fingered the letters, closed my eyes, thought of Bell making love to the little man. I swayed a little, bumped my head. Bell turned down the radio and said, "Who's there?" in a frightened voice.

"It's me, let me in." I heard him go into the bathroom, open the medicine chest, pause, close it, then walk down the hall to the door. Bell pulled back the dead bolt. He smiled when he saw me.

"Why so serious, Jesse?" he asked. He was wearing the silk kimono, one arm pulled in tightly as if it were sprained. The skin around his eyes was a greasy gray from wearing mascara and removing it with vaseline.

"Well?" he asked. "Did you quit?"

When I nodded he was so relieved his face smoothed and he let out an easy breath. He led me like a child down the hall, all the time keeping his shoulder up and his arm pressed against his side. The place smelled of garlic and burning wax and I saw the big cement lawn statue of Jesus on the black table and the candles lit around it.

"Having a seance?" I asked.

Bell didn't answer. He sat at the table, rifling through a shoe box full of seeds, picking up a packet of sunflowers, then zinnias, reading the tiny instructions on the back. A Chinese newspaper was spread all over the floor and taped to the walls. There was nowhere to sit. The couch springs were uncovered. I eyed the closet and the rumpled futon.

"Ah, lovely," Bell said, and held up a packet of blue morning glory seeds. He ripped the top off and rattled the contents into his mouth, then swigged from his pint bottle of gin. "I've decided to grow a garden in my stomach."

"Your heart will think it's found a soulmate," I said.

Bell smiled, looked over my head. His eyes focused on the tiny Chinese characters and his lips moved as if he could read them. His forehead wrinkled and he leaned toward me, clamping his cool hand over my wrist. The candle flames showed themselves in each of his eyes and I remembered when we used to joke that he was the devil. He motioned with his head for me to move closer and whispered, "Keep your plans secret for now." I was startled, not sure whether to admit my rental car was waiting outside, that I was anxious to get on the road, anxious to finally meet Kevin. But he didn't continue, just looked into the street as if he might see someone that could save his life. The lamp on the floor cast him in pathetic light. Bell stood, his kimono opened and he asked me if I'd like a drink. His nude body seemed yellow and swollen, with a fine coating of sweat that smelled of juniper berries. He'd been drinking for days. I stared at the texture of his balls, their fragility had always startled me. It seemed men were hostile and mean to protect that vulnerable spot, not to celebrate their hard cocks. He went into the kitchen, opened the refrigerator. The ice cubes fell into the sink and onto the floor.

"I want you to stop all this wallowing."

He turned suddenly and even in the shadowy kitchen I could see his face fill with pain. "I killed my father," he said, his hurt arm tighter as if it was meant to hold him up. "He wanted a haircut. So my mother took him into town to the barbershop. He urged her to leave, he wanted to be alone with the men. When she came back he was waiting outside, shivering. The men teased him, said his son was a faggot." He left his mouth open, raised his eyebrows, as if to say, isn't that incredible, I killed my father.

"It's still not your fault."

"It is!" he said, squinting at me, trying to see me as a memory years from now. He wanted to be responsible for his father's death. He'd rather revel in some tragic poignancy than his regular mundane life. It reminded me of my own melancholy about my parents' divorce. Weeks ago he might have convinced me it was noble, not now. Bell's father was dead and he hadn't seen Kevin for ten years and it was ridiculous for him to be this way. I stood, walked into the dark kitchen, put my arms loosely around his neck and tried to ease him into my body. But he pulled away, reached his hand under his stiff arm and took out a medium-size speckled egg. "I'm going to hatch it," he said, walking to the table holding the egg down close to the candle-light. "That purple color means it won't be long now," he said, tucking the egg back under his arm, pressing his elbow against his side. "Is there anything more delicate than an egg?" he asked smiling.

"Yeah," I said. "Relationships."

Bell looked at me in a blank way that made me sure it was time to leave. "We should get married," he said. "My father would love you."

THE RENTAL CAR HAD A DASHBOARD OF WARM GREEN LIGHT. The interior smelled of the immortality of plastic. The engine was quiet and it seemed more like my mind that pushed me forward than the cylinders of exploding gasoline. The headlights made people on the street momentarily transparent and that image of a face fading away as if from memory got me thinking of Bell, and about how little one person can help another. I'd tried to convince him he wasn't responsible for his father's death and give him some possibility of a future. But the only future I was willing to work for was one together. I could only save him through his commitment to me. And Bell was gay, or at least ambivalent enough to make the idea of marriage ridiculous. But even if I were a man, as I often used to wish, I couldn't stop him from going down. It was what he wanted. I could tell by the way he held his cigarette, how when he spoke he looked coldly through my head and into the next world.

I felt guilty. If I'd ever really loved him, I should have stayed nearby. But I couldn't decide whether it was stronger to leave him or to stay and help. I remembered my mother's face, puffy from crying after Dad left. She took both my hands into hers and said, "Promise me that if you are ever treated badly you will leave." I only wish all her crazy oaths and advice wouldn't rise so often in my mind. But it was more than that, I was sick of Bell and Madison and Pig and all of San Francisco, sick of being nice, being nurturing, being a good sport, of appeasing people. I started to think of maggots festering in a wound. I thought of betraying people who loved me, of piss and shit mixed foully in a backed-up toilet. I figured if I knew exactly what I wanted then maybe I'd stop being so polite and that's why I had to speak with Kevin. But what did he know about my crazy ideas of love and family—intensified by my parents' divorce and my own faithless life? I thought about the story my mother often told of reaching for my father in bed and him saying, "Don't embarrass yourself." Could I blame this whole thing on them, on their divorce? Even as a child I was insecure and sneaky. I always needed a huge amount of attention and I often pretended to be sick or stupid to get it. I'd been the little actress and had not lived the right life from the start.

I grabbed the wheel so hard my knuckles whitened and a pain shot into my palm. I accelerated, mesmerized by the red taillights. I understood in an atavistic way the idea of murder, how frustration, fury and pain could be catharted momentarily by doing something horrible. I turned my signal on, eased into the middle lane, the tick and blink hypnotized me. I wondered if I was going to L.A. to kill Kevin.

I felt his long fingers reaching into my skull. The equation went like this: Bell + Kevin and Jesse + Bell = Jesse vs. Kevin. To think of him leaning toward me, that first deep smell of his body. I imagined him slipping away from his reception to meet me at a hotel, a champagne bottle under his tux jacket, a piece of his wedding cake stuffed into my mouth. As he pulled down my panties he'd say he liked the idea of betraying his wife on their wedding day, that it was poignant and true. I tried to think of when Kevin and Bell were together in Chinatown for the new year: lanterns, the long paper dragon zigzagging over the street, the firecrackers. Bell told me that afterward they'd gone for a drink to a gay bar. He'd brushed his hand against Kevin's cock, both of them laughing and flushed like children.

The road narrowed past Half Moon Bay, and the regularity of houses diminished. The sea was black and the mountains blue in the moonlight. Occasionally I'd see a low California-style ranch, dark except for the glow of a blue TV. America is America, I thought, because of the things we do together. The road soothed me, the water gently shifting, like someone stroking my hair. I turned on the radio but all I could find were men talking about the probability of war and a religious talk show.

A man and a woman talked about AIDS education, how the literature was a how-to manual for homosexuality, how celibacy was the only answer now.

I thought of the Pacific, of the crabs and fish that lived underneath the surface. The Atlantic seemed dirty, even scrawny in comparison. When I first came to California, it seemed a clichéd utopia where people took endless vitamins, spoke with gurus, spiritual healers, herbalists, accepted karma as a reality. I resented their spiritual superiority and didn't care much whether Nostradamus was right and that an earthquake might send the hippies, surfers, movie stars, right-wingers toppling into the sea. I imagined the wreckage washed up on the Nevada coast: crocheted hats, tie-dye, skateboards, love beads. But out here, closer to the land, I realized how the West Coast balanced the East.

JUST BEFORE MONTEREY MY HEADLIGHTS ILLUMINATED A GIRL walking quickly down the soft shoulder. She was wearing tight jeans and a T-shirt and was rubbing her hands over her bare arms. She was so young, I wondered why she was out so late. I slowed but she didn't look up. She seemed upset, like after a fight with a boyfriend. There were headlights in my rearview mirror so I sped ahead. Her short hair and sullen sexy walk reminded me of the girls I'd admired in high school, the ones who did everything first. In the rearview mirror I watched the car stop, the driver was an older man. When she got in there was a pouting curve to her hips that told me he was not her father.

They passed me easily. She leaned into him, her hair caught in the wind.

The highway into Monterey degenerated into a strip. It was too late for anything to be open. On the main stretch were gift shops, the slightly upscale kind, that sold driftwood art and watercolor paintings. Down the road was the aquarium, and all that was left of Cannery Row. There were lots of T-shirt places, a few antique stores, a place that sold kites, one for wind chimes. There was a McDonald's and a Taco Bell and a restaurant called the Grapes of Wrath . . . like everywhere else in America that was special, it had been spoiled by gentrification.

Just outside the village it started to rain, so I decided to stop at a little hotel I saw on the bluff to my left. I drove up, parked my car beside a VW van—the only other car in the lot. The rain was harder now, beating on the pavement and on me as I dashed into the office. The fluorescent lights buzzed and the muted sound of rain was cozy, made me glad I'd stopped. The place had the intimate aroma of sweat and curry and was shabby, with cracked leather couches and a bucket near the desk catching a melody of drips from the stained ceiling. There was a noise in the back room and simultaneously an Indian man pulled back the beaded curtains that separated the back room from this one. He looked sleepy and his shiny hair stuck up in the back like a bird. He was barefoot and his brown pants and white T-shirt were wrinkled. I saw his wife in the slit of the curtain, curled on the bed, her long hair spread out over the pillow. She wore a red dot on her forehead and I imagined her in a golden sari, on a blue California day, straining leaves with a long pole from the pool outside. The man pointed at a handwritten sign under the glass of the counter. I handed him twenty dollars and he gave me a room key.

Outside, I stood under the awning, the clouds gave the sky a grayish purple tone and rain blew across my face. It was chilly and I walked toward my room. The curtain of Room 8 was slightly parted and the TV was on. I could see a man and a woman in one of the two double beds. A pattern of light and shadow showed the woman's head nuzzled into the man's hair, his arm thrown back to touch her waist. The curtain of my room was closed, but I could see through that the TV was on. This scared me and I started back toward the office, but the light was off and I knew the man was back in bed with his wife.

I opened my door quickly, checked under each bed and behind the shower curtain. The linoleum in the bathroom was rolling up in the corners and the tub had a greasy film. The carpet in the main room was bright red and riddled with a constellation of cigarette burns. There was no window in the back, just an old air conditioner jutting from the paneled walls. There were paintings over the beds of ghost ships, and near the TV was a pressed-wood table and a dresser that matched. The sound was off on the TV. The place reminded me of a porno movie with the red bed and creepy light. The anxious face of the TV announcer spoke emphatically, then the picture switched to footage of a mother helping her children put on gas masks. I flung myself down on the bed, and with my fingertips rubbed at the tense muscles in my neck. The woman on TV sealed the door shut with electrical tape and put a plastic cover over her baby's crib. The announcer spoke silently and then they showed the enemy capital, bombs bursting over its domes and onion-shaped towers. I made myself imagine the people there who were dying, the way their bodies would be twisted, the sounds in the streets. The horror. The TV flashed black planes and white missiles and grainy footage of a bomb hitting its target like a video game. A cat outside started to cry. I closed my eyes, but all I could see were the headlights from my rearview mirror. I pulled the bedspread back, pulled off my shirt, unlatched my bra, but left my pants on, and pulled the covers over me. I kissed my pillow and pulled it into my chest like a lover.

I couldn't sleep and ended up thinking back on all my men. I hadn't been a nice girl, but it didn't have anything to do with sex, more to do with lying. With each man I acted identically, like a ritual. I started by alluding to our life a few years ahead, then ten, then twenty. I'd joke about our children's names, tell him what a feisty old guy he'd be at eighty. It would escalate, we'd speak of buying houses together, joining bank accounts. When I got pregnant once, I'd kept it secret, then aborted. Sometimes someone new would lead me to break it off so quickly and absolutely the guy would be dazed, even shocked, as if I were insane. One man broke into my apartment and read my journals, ripped the crotch out of all my panties. Another followed me across the country, appeared with flowers and a new car begging me to run away. But I had already started up with someone new, was telling him my sad childhood stories. Saying, We wouldn't raise our baby that way. For me a relationship has never been possible unless it was going to end in marriage and children and forever. My heart beat furiously, I cupped my tit, pressed my fingers against my breastbone so I could feel my heart heaving up into my palm. The woman in the next room was talking and I imagined myself snuggled between the lovers in that spot between his warm belly and her smooth back, the lattice of her spine. It was so comfortable there that I soon fell asleep.

A car engine woke me in the deepest part of the night. I went to the window, saw the back lights of the van, the lovers curving down the bluff toward the highway. The TV had changed to bright vertical stripes. I saw my body in its light, my skin was looser than I remembered. It seemed incredible I'd been a baby, that my body could have a child, that someday I'd be old and that someday I'd be dead. I turned off the TV, remembering the sensation of being between the lovers, realized how precious two bodies were when warm and settled side by side.

IN THE MORNING IT SEEMED CRAZY I WAS ON THIS PILGRIMAGE and at around ten when I saw the lovers' VW van parked on the grassy shoulder I decided to stop, parked my car, sat inside for a moment. Mounds of moss-green water moved endlessly toward the shore. When the waves rose up and thinned I could see black seaweed inside them like my glass paperweight with the rose encased inside. I walked out through the long grass, down the rocky incline to the water.

I knelt by a tidal pool. Starfish clung to the bottom,

radiant in shades of purple and fuchsia. I picked one off a rock and was surprised at its fleshiness. There were sea urchins, too, and a luminescent seaweed. As I reached down to touch those slippery strains, I saw the lovers clung together. Surprised into stillness, averting my eyes, I was like a deer that hopes incomprehension and inaction will render it invisible. One time I was with a boy on a river bank when car lights flashed across the water and illuminated my body. It was a familiar female equation, abandon changed quickly to shame.

My foot slid forward several steps on the slimy rocks. She was on top with both hands on the ground, so all I saw were the man's quivering legs and her humping ass. Their intensity made me conscious of the blood moving through me and the geometry of my bones. The waves seemed far away like the ocean heard in a hand-held shell. It was creepy the way I had tracked them.

The women turned her head and saw me. Her eyes were obsidian and lips bluish and pellucid like a shell. She turned back to her lover, sunk into his chest and gave him a long open-mouthed kiss. The lovers seemed a natural part of the scene. It showed me how freakish I'd become. The sensation terrified me and I ran back to the car, revved the engine, skidded onto the highway and drove toward L.A.

Chapter

Eleven

ON THE EDGE OF L.A. I STOPPED AT A GAS STATION, BOUGHT A map and asked the mechanic if he would show me how to get to the church. He drew a twisty blue snake that curved as I did now through the canyons. To either side stood single-story homes with lots of glass, additions like robotic arms jutting from the back. The yards were neatly overgrown, voluptuous with palmettos and bougainvillea. The church stood on a cul-de-sac overlooking a highway. It was a sprawling single-story complex that contained a bowling alley and a health club. On the wall nearest me was a mosaic: L.A. Jesus, hair blown back, lips parted. The highway below hummed, and though the sky was blue, the light was dusty and brownish yellow, making the church look barren and radioactive.

I hadn't slept much last night, and the wedding was still several hours away, so I bunched up my coat and lay over the

front seat. At first I thought of the lovers. Death, actual or
metaphorical, was the logical conclusion to most love affairs.
The only other alternative was some sort of permanent unity,
that's why I had to speak with Kevin. I thought of this L.A.
suburbia . . . shot in the arm with Hollywood's cash and
confidence . . . the highway lulled me, sounded like water, like
rain. I remembered when I was a kid, the deep hole in my
backyard. There was water at the bottom and I would squat on
the lip, listening to the sloshing echoes, watching the light on
the water like a black mirror. I heard a car engine start down the
block. My mind drifted up, floated like a piece of paper to a hill
where I used to sled. I was wearing a green prom dress, one I
knew from a picture of my mother with a boy named John from
West Point. My mother wished she had married that boy. My
grandmother told me that when he heard she was serious with
someone else he came down from school and they sat on the
back porch. John told her it didn't matter if they raised the kids
Catholic, the kids could be Protestant, but they should get
married. "It's been settled," my mother said. "I'm going to be
a minister's wife." The taffeta chafed under my arm and I was
in Dolores Park on the hill above the tennis courts. At the
bottom I could see my house in Virginia, my mother in the front
window, all dark except the TV's blue light showing the outline
of her slip and her beefy legs folded under. I started to run,
hoping the wind would pick me up. This seemed perfectly
possible. The smell of grass was everywhere and wood smoke
too, and the world was a ragged strip of green to either side. My
feet were just lifting when I saw a pale-haired minister in a black

suit and clerical collar. Instead of a Bible he was holding a *Playboy* magazine. I rose up again, heard the cars on the highway, moved my shoulder which was getting stiff. The minister spoke: "Love is a rare possession, almost inane and unnatural these days. It is associated with pleasure, but it is no stranger to pain." His whole face caved in and I took his hand and was surprised that my own wasn't an adult hand but the babyish one of a five-year-old. He told me jealousy was really the dark twin of duty, that he was so jealous, he looked through the dirty laundry, checking his wife's underwear for sperm stains. We walked into a pine forest, the rust-colored needles snapping under our feet and the evergreens swaying like hay fields. "And forgive those who have trespassed, those who have lusted, those who have lied," the minister said and he looked at me then. His eye sockets were empty; I could see straight through his head to the green trees. I loved the man because I knew he held a little chapel in his heart and then suddenly I was inside. The air was humid and beyond the stained glass I could see blood moving in patterns like water. At the altar was a bride and groom. Even from behind they looked familiar, it was my parents, flushed, stupidly happy. A convoy of trucks down on the highway rocked my car and I woke. There was organ music and when I lifted my head I saw the sun setting, and that I was surrounded with cars, that the bride was standing with her father just outside the open doors. She was lovely in her creamy satin gown, light glinting the beadwork on her train. Her father, a thin terse man who reminded me of a general, took her arm under his. The music rose louder and they stepped into the church. I thought of my mother's voice saying I was attracted to the same kind of bums as my father, "You'll be dumped at forty-five too." I watched the last bit of white lace slither inside and someone's hands reach out and pull both doors shut.

I PASSED CARS GOING SEVENTY, BLEW MY HORN FOR NO REASON, screamed at a man who tried to pass me. I thought of how a doctor had once suggested boric acid for my yeast infection, the same stuff I used to kill roaches in my apartment.

I got lost, drove into West Hollywood, then onto Sunset Strip. I chain-smoked cigarettes, lighting each new one off the bitter end of the last, I had a stray-dog feeling that made me want to do something loose and crazy and I was: crashing a reception, confronting the groom about his homosexual past—asking like a child about *love.* It was dark, though I could still see the studio complexes set back from the road, underlit and surrounded with a lattice of barbed-wire fences. The area outside was tacky with restaurants, gift shops and a variety of businesses that each claimed to be the home of the stars.

I zigzagged through side roads, saw men feeding sticks into a fire in a trash can. Homeboys wearing pukka beads hung out at the corners in nylon jogging suits. To join some gangs you had to kill someone and I remembered the crazy college boy who had offered to murder someone for me. He said it wouldn't be murder because the person would be sacrificed. How many times had my mother said she sacrificed her life for mine? And I had fed off her, bolstered my own self-worth in accordance with her misery. My father got strength from demeaning her, too—making rude comments about her weight, saying he was going to trade her in for two twenty-year-olds. When he said that we were all in the TV room, the smell of hamburgers and cheese was still in the air from dinner. No one gained emotional power without someone else losing some.

I found my way back onto the freeway and headed toward Beverly Hills. The red taillights made me dreamy and I thought of the glowing tip of Bell's cigarette and wondered if he was checking his egg to see if the baby bird was breaking through. Or was he in his father's gabardine shirt, hair slicked back, a hint of eyeliner, slowly smoking a clove cigarette, anticipating the back room of the White Swallow. Madison was easier. She'd be passed out, sprawled across her furry bedspread, the bartender downstairs checking the beer supply, wiping dust off the liquor bottles. Madison hears the water from the fish tanks, dreams she is a mermaid, but then there's a noise from the street and she remembers a man is coming at eight who likes to be shit on and one at nine who pretends she is his daughter. She wonders if it might be true even now, that women were made for the pleasure of others.

I FOUND MY WAY BACK INTO BEVERLY HILLS, MERCEDES AND Porsche dealerships stood on every corner surrounded by palm trees and flowers. Tan people in pastels were radiant in the dark. Was it the soft light? The modernistic architecture? The air itself, heavily scented with smog? What made L.A. look like a touched-up photograph, like a set with actors waiting for the director to yell *Cut?*

The hotel was a cream-colored stucco building with a red tile roof. A mix of Mexican and Hollywood, the Zorro style. I parked the car on clean asphalt beside orderly flower beds. The moon was a perfect half, as if sliced with a razor. Inside the door was a fireplace with a ceramic log throwing up gas flames. I followed the signs to the back room and made my way into the reception. The wedding party wasn't here, but the room was full of men and women in suits and formal dresses sitting at round tables. A Western chandelier made from several wagon wheels hung over them. Women in black-and-white uniforms carried in silver trays of food and set them on a long table in front near the white tiered cake. The bartender poured buckets of ice into his cooler. He was thin with a capsule-shaped head and acne that resembled diaper rash. I walked over and ordered a double bourbon, listened to a couple talk: she said his brain was in his cock. I carried the drink back to my table, the white tablecloth felt stiff under my fingers and the roses in the middle were so lovely they looked fake.

I watched a pair of young women in silk dresses and soft leather shoes move along the hors d'oeuvres table. They laughed, confident that this whole ritual would be repeated for them. Their natural inclusion made me feel like the witch at the christening in Sleeping Beauty. But I couldn't leave. The thought of the suspended blowfish at Madison's spinning slowly in the street light, and of Bell passed out across the bed, and of the lovers too, the pink crevice of her rear, the muscles flexing in the man's hairy thighs . . . My hand shook. I thought of talking to Kevin, the one person who could save Bell. But even if Kevin did agree to come, he wouldn't—I couldn't even ask— what good would it do? Maybe at first Bell would be hopeful, but Kevin would eventually leave and Bell would be alone again and worse off because, like Pig, his center memory would be skewed.

I went back to the bar. It was more crowded; standing in back of a man in a pinstripe suit I smelled his lime aftershave, his stale smell of cigarettes. Men smell of the world, the street. Women smell domesticated, of the garden, spice. The wilder ones of animal musk or opium. When it was my turn, I ordered two double bourbons. The bartender looked up, I told him one was for a friend. On the walk back, I watched the bourbon eat the ice cubes. My vision was fuzzy near the edge. I sat down; an older couple was seated across from me. The plump woman pushed her chest out toward her tiny husband who reminded me of dehydrated food. I picked a rose from the centerpiece and put it in my hair. The woman watched me, suspicious of my jeans and high-top tennis shoes, but I didn't care. Everything was easing, seemed funny and right. The ceiling fans had some- thing to do with the meaning of life. A murmur ran through the crowd, then scattered applause. The bride walked in holding her dress up with both hands. She stopped at a table of blue-haired ladies. Kevin was behind her, there was no mistaking those eyes, the same winter-sky blue as Bell's and his light brown hair hung at his shoulders and was very clean like a girl's. Kevin went to a table of young men in well-cut suits and colorful ties. One said

something about a ball and chain and they all laughed. I rose off
my seat, tried to motion to him, but there was the old lady's eyes
and I realized it was a drunken move. I felt suddenly shy. What
could it be like to be so loved? They moved together up to their
table, groomsmen and bridesmaids behind them and with much
joking and laughing they all took their seats. A man, similar to
Kevin, maybe a brother, opened a bottle of champagne.

The women carried in deeper trays of food and set them
over sterno burners. The band picked up a little, played "String
of Pearls." The general came and asked his daughter to dance.
Kevin went and got his mother-in-law. Others from the wedding party joined in. It was all a blur of satin and silk. I stood,
walked to the bar to get another drink. The ceiling seemed too
low and it was more difficult than I remembered to get by the
chairs. The boy poured me another and I carried it to the dance
floor, stood on the edge watching Kevin dance with a bridesmaid. Her purple chiffon skirt swayed out. I imagined him and
Bell, the afternoon they'd both put on make-up and listened to
"Satellite of Love." Bell worshiped Kevin, his prophetic-youth-
ful insights, his teenage body. And through me, Bell's desire was
still strong. I waited until he was at arm's length, slugged my
drink back, dropped the plastic cup on the floor and tapped the
bridesmaid's shoulder. She smiled, stepped away. Kevin put a
hand to my waist and moved me forward with the music. He
squinted his eyes as if reading in bad light, but he couldn't place
me and asked if I'd gotten in late and was I a friend of Maria's
from college.

"I'm Jesse," I said.

He stopped.

"He still loves you."

Kevin looked sheepishly to either side, then tucked his head and whispered that I should meet him in a few minutes in Suite 33. He pulled away from me, walked out tersely, head down, obviously shaken. I stood for a dazed moment on the dance floor, then walked back to my table. I tried to decide what I'd say, but it was too hot and my mind wandered. It was a relief to leave the stuffy room and stand in the cooler cowboy-style lobby. The elevator door opened and I got in. In the mirror that covered the walls my face looked like a murderer's, pale with evil resignation. I realized I was supposed to have a gun, that it was stupid to talk to Kevin, that I'd come to kill him. At three I got out and walked the beige-carpeted hallway and knocked on 33. The door opened, Kevin grabbed my wrist and pulled me inside. "This is crazy," he said.

I sat on one of the double beds. The spreads were deep blue and there was a vase of white roses and a basket of wax fruit on the night table. He was voluptuous with his puffy lips and long thick hair.

"He's obsessed with you still," I said to Kevin who watched me uneasily, rolling up his sleeves, rattling his cuff links like dice.

"Bell loves to spend all his time desiring things. It gives him an excuse whenever he fails." He looked like he might go on, but he shook his head. "I can't have you here," he said. "It makes me nervous."

"I'm no threat to you," I said.

"Are you kidding?" Kevin said, running his hand through his hair.

"I came here to ask you about love." It sounded so stupid, I looked down while I said it.

"Like I'm some sort of expert?" He shook his head. We were small and ghostly on the TV screen.

"You just married a woman, you must be in love."

"Bell's ideas poison everything," he said. "You have to forget you met him. Don't you see how he's miserable, how he wants you to be miserable too?"

I was startled. "How can you say that?"

Kevin walked over to me and sat at the edge of the bed. "You gotta fall into the river. Know what I mean?"

I was touched at this naive advice and told him how once my mother had come into my room in the middle of the night and said that sex was messy, that sperm ran down your legs. He stared, thinking I was crazy, hoping I would leave.

"You must go," he said. "I cannot help you." I felt a little sorry for him, just half an hour ago he'd married.

"I'll go if you tell me about the first time with Bell."

He flushed. "That's private."

"If you tell me I'll leave," I said.

"It was in school," he said.

"And?"

"You'll definitely go?"

I nodded.

He put his hand on his forehead and stared into the gray TV. Everything around him was straight angles; the bed, the nightstand, the chair by the wall. This was hard for him. "I don't remember why but we were the only ones. Bell came over to my desk and asked me to stand. He rubbed his pencil longways back and forth over my penis. Then we snuck out and into the bathroom. He showed me how we could lock ourselves in the stall and balance on the toilet so nobody could see our feet. He put his palms against the wall and let me take him from behind."

The thought of them suspended—hands, legs, their heads at odds but balanced—reminded me of an atom, of the three-dimensional models I saw in school. And that moment *was* Bell's first lightning bolt of life, connected even now to his every molecule.

I stood. "I'll be leaving now if you'll kiss me?" He leaned back as if the thought disgusted him, but then he looked at me and said, "You're really on your way out?"

I nodded and his hot mouth was suddenly over mine. I didn't like his teeth, sharp like a rat and his thin lips seemed like they had bones. He pressed his scaly tongue into my mouth. I slipped my hand over his pants, felt his cock tightening, bowing, as Bell had said, to the left. Happy people are the cruelest, I thought. This was the cock Bell wanted in his mouth, up his ass. Kevin stopped kissing me and brushed my hand away from his pants.

"You can't tell where you stop and other people start," he said. "That's a dangerous quality to have."

Chapter

Twelve

THE DESERT SUNRISE FILLED MY HEAD. THE LIGHT STALKING ME, a sunrise as certain as the end of the world. Mid-afternoon I arrived, parked the car on Polk Street and dropped the keys through the rental office mail slot. Walking up the shady side of Bush I felt like my head was filled with fiberglass. I wanted to see Bell and the futon. I planned to sleep so long and deeply that when I woke, it would be as if from a past life.

Traffic was light on Bush, a rumpled couple just out of bed passed me, and a homeless man checked trash bins for aluminum cans. Like dream fractals, everything echoed my mood: the pattern in the sidewalk, shapes in the clouds, an image in a stranger's eye. Maybe it was the patina of guilt. I'd done something dishonest in going to Kevin's wedding and I wanted to tell Bell. On the corner of Taylor I paused at the light, took in the used-book store and the fire station across from Bell's apartment.

Someone grabbed my arm, and I jumped, turned to see the little man, his eyes bulging under thick glasses.

"I've been looking for you everywhere."

"I've been busy," I said blankly, hoping callousness might send him away.

"I know," he said, adjusting his glasses. "Bell doesn't answer the door."

"He's probably wandered off."

The little man shook his head. "I would have seen him."

He was worried. I could see it in his runny eggish eyes, the way he looked spasmodically to Bell's door.

"Do you love him?"

"It's more than we both understand."

"Have you fucked him?" I asked.

"He wouldn't after I told him, as a child, I put my teddy bear in the oven."

It was the kind of bad omen that would make perfect sense to Bell.

"What I can't figure," he said, his face pinched with curiosity, "is what's so special about you? You see, Bell thinks it's much more exciting with men, he feels like a little boy. With women, he's painting a picture, idolizes the image, falls for it, like one falls for a character in a novel." The little man paused, flipped his head to Bell's building. "Let me tell you your future."

"Fuck you," I said.

The little man hunched his shoulders and turned. "Mark my word. I'm never wrong." He ran down Taylor Street, staying close to the building like a rat.

The sun reflected like fire on the top windows of Bell's building and the bricks turned a peachy pink color. My key slid open the door. The foyer was dark, smelling faintly of roses and garlic. The worn Victorian atmosphere was so appealing after the antiseptic rawness of L.A. There was Indian music coming from the other end of Bell's floor and someone had left a bunch of bags near the garbage chute.

"Bell," I said, as my key met with the lock and the dead bolt gave. I called his name again, pushed the door open and walked down the hall, passed the bathroom door and the telephone table. The couch, jade plant, even the futon seemed miniaturized, like going back to a childhood home. Standing there, I could tell he wasn't home and hadn't been all day. The bed was made. His calico scallop shells were arranged by size on the windowsill. His altar in order, postcards of cathedrals, glass candle holders. He'd swept, left a pile of dirt, dust balls, hair, lint and pennies. There were no dirty glasses in the sink and he'd put the silverware away in their proper compartments. Even the splattered spaghetti sauce had been wiped from the tiles over the stove.

I took a pillow from the bed and ducked into the closet, sat on Bell's summer bucks, leaned against the side wall. From here I could see the vault of light retreating out the window. When I thought of what Kevin had said, that I couldn't tell the difference between myself and others, I knew he was right. It was a quality my mother had, Madison and Pig too. Most women ended in blurs and fragments, but that wasn't really a bad thing. I remembered how Kevin's jaw clicked and as he stepped away from me I was certain he would hit me. He didn't know that you slept with your lover's past and future lovers and those lovers' lovers. My hand on his dick angered him because he realized in the midst of the simplicity of his wedding, the clarity of his union, that life was hopelessly complicated.

Bell only wandered when he was depressed. He would complain about the vague unhappiness of life. He was sad he wasn't famous. Though he told me, once you knew you could be famous, it didn't matter if you were. Bell knew not to complain, everyone loves a martyr. I thought of happy endings, how novelists usually flinched. To admit your characters are doomed means you are too.

The familiar smell of our clothes made me sleepy, it was dark and I could still hear the Indian music, a sitar drawing me toward sleep, it was an anxious lonely sleep. I was walking south of Market toward the Bay Bridge, paper blew against a chain-link fence and I realized how empty the city seemed. I stuck my thumb out, pressed my hips forward, saw a car ahead I knew would stop for me. The man behind the wheel reminded me of someone, though I couldn't remember who. He asked me how far I was going, but I didn't answer. I saw myself in his sunglasses, transparent, held together only by his gaze.

* * *

WHEN I WOKE IT WAS DARK, THE HOTEL HUNTINGTON'S LIGHT dammed at the curtains. I crawled over shoes, through Bell's cashmere coat and curled up under the comforter. With my knees touching my chin I drifted down, then heard the sound of water dripping. Not to porcelain like a leaky faucet, but falling into other water. Plup. Plup. Plup. Bell must have come in while I was asleep and drawn himself a bath. I pressed my ear against the wall, listening for his breath, or the classical tape—the *Jupiter* Symphony or some boys' choir. Nothing. I sat up. Should I wait for him to come to bed? Pretend to talk in my sleep? It's been two weeks since I dyed my hair. I stood and walked on my tiptoes down the hall. There was light coming from under the door, bright as a laser. "Bell," I said, "I know you're in there." He didn't answer. Maybe he'd found out I was at the wedding? Maybe Kevin had called? "I want to talk to you." Still no answer. He pissed me off, using his silence to emasculate me, make me feel vulnerable. "I touched Kevin's dick," I said. Plup. Plup. No swish of water, no long fed-up sigh.

I put my hand on the knob and pushed the door, letting it creak open. There was Bell's head tipped back over the edge of the tub. He must be drunk. I saw the red water, how Bell's right arm floated palm up, how he'd sliced his arm from elbow to hand, the open skin evocative as a mouth. The other arm hung over the tub's edge, blood streaked his hand, congealed in a puddle fed by his fingertips. He was strangely beautiful with pale white skin, blue eyes, purple lips, and on his cheeks a soft spot of pink rouge. I felt weak, nauseated, then so hot I took off my sweater. My ears began ringing, sweat rose under my clothes. I leaned over the toilet and puked. Yellow bile that swirled in the bowl, the bitter taste of lead.

I screamed. My vocal cords quivered and stung. Louder so the sitar stopped, so the sound swallowed me, Bell, the apartment, the block. I used to kiss his lower stomach, the warm hair around his cock. I'd put an ear to his skin and hear liquid sloshing in his bladder, his heart beating. His body was proof of *life* to me.

I leaned against the sink, turned the glass knob until cold water beat from the faucet. I let the water wash over my wrist, then put my head under, wet the hair at the back of my neck until I got chills. There were blank spots where I stared at the water swirling around the drain, the hair curling on the porcelain, and remembered my first morning with Bell, how I wrapped a sheet around me and came into this room and how my pee was warm, stinging from sex. I squeezed in between the toilet and the wall. The room reeked of bile and blood. I could tell by his wrinkled skin that he had done this last night, about the time Kevin said his vows. Bell's head was turned slightly toward me, so I could see only one eye. As a child he had learned that remoteness drew people to him, but this had proven dangerous. The tile was cool on my spine and I looked into his unyielding eye. He wasn't meant to be a groom, or a father, or even a son. He was meant to be dead. And in death he was mine. He used to tell me that a person who reads all day, then watches the sunset is just as valuable as a person who interacts with the world, but he didn't believe it and God knows this world doesn't either.

My life fans out like a string of paper dolls. I am malleable, chameleonlike. Each life eats the last until I'm a Russian doll, containing ten women of decreasing size.

Across the desert, the midlands, creeping back into the South. To Virginia where you can feel the water in the pages of a book and the light rain makes the leaves tender as skin. I will plant a rose garden and I will wait in that garden for the flick of the snake's tongue that will change me again.

On the tub's shiny faucet, the distorted image of my face floated above the toilet. Watching Bell's unblinking eye I brought my hand to my mouth, kissed the palm deeply, wet tongue against the ridges of my lifeline.

If he died for my sins, I am grateful.